S F
BOOKS

SPARK & FIZZ BOOKS PRESENTS

PLANET SCUMM

WINTER 2020   "A BLOODY PULP"   ISSUE NO. 9

— A SANGUINE TABLE OF CONTENTS —

TRANSMISSION: SCUMM
HOSTED BY THE SCUMM BUDS..V

AUTHOR BIOS..XI

BRAIN TRUST
HAILEY PIPER..1

AHEAD OF DRAGONS
DAVID BUSBOOM..13

ON THE ORIGIN OF FEAR
CLARISSA VAN DELL..20

SIERRA STARFALL AND THE ELDERS OF THE SPACEWAYS
PEDRO INIGUEZ..31

MARIGOLDS IN WINTER
ELENA SICHROVSKY..48

A SONG FOR GANYMEDE
AUSTIN P. SHEEHAN..54

ARTIST SPOTLIGHTS..71

EDITOR IN CHIEF	CREATIVE DIRECTOR	MANAGING EDITOR	EDITOR	EDITOR
SEAN CLANCY	*ALYSSA ALARCÓN SANTO*	*TYLER BERD*	*ERIC LOUCKS*	*SAM RHEAUME*

COVER BY ALYSSA ALARCÓN SANTO | @ALYSSASANTODESIGN   SPOT ART BY SAM RHEAUME | @SIRHEAUME

Planet Scumm is a triannual short fiction anthology. Visit **planetscumm.space** for submissions.

© SPARK & FIZZ BOOKS
Portland | Boston | New York

First Printing, 2020   ISBN: 978-1-970154-06-1

TRANSMISSION: SCUMM

SCUMM MEMORIAL JELLYTHON

◆

...the sound's weird? Nah, I have it right here. Muffled? Well, yeah it's muffled—I ate it. I said I ate the mic. The mic's insid—oh slime it all, we're back on!

Wasn't that thing you were just listening to great folks? I certainly assume it was. You're receiving—whether you want to or not—"Planet Scumm," the *only* moon-sized broadcast station and doomsday weapon this side of Andromeda.

Smiley Scumm here, big-mouthed bloviator and one of *many* budding byproducts born from the blasted body of our forbear, Scummy.

We're here in hour 4,387 of the Memorial Jellython, honoring our departed leader with non-stop singled-celled sonic shenanigans. Speaking of hours—the chronometer floating in my cytoplasm tells me it's time to check in with some stories from around the galaxy.

First up—brains. Even a puffed-up, evolutionarily anachronistic slimeball like myself knows they're important. Whether you use them for mental noodling or you serve them over noodles, seems like anyone who's *anyone* needs a few on hand these days. But the brain trend isn't a recent phenomena. Hailey Piper gives us some historical context in ***"Brain Trust,"*** tracing the popularity of cerebrum collections all the way back to pre-radio Earth.

Oh, what those lovable, delicious little humans will get themselves into! I don't have the patience to raise any myself, but after *Planet Scumm's* taboo-shattering (and continent-shattering) visit to the Earther planet last cycle, many galactic residents have found themselves the proud new owners of Earther colonies. David Busboom covers that development in ***"Ahead of Dragons,"*** and shows us that even technologically-advanced civilizations can learn a thing or two from earthers about love and counterinsurgency.

Folks, don't you want to just get away from it all sometimes? Just... take a single-seat fighter out to an isolated asteroid, park 'er in a clammy cave, and chill for a few aeons until the Intergalactic Criminal Court dissolves? We've all had that feeling. But for the deserter in Clarissa Van Dell's ***"On the Origin of Fear,"*** a trip to an isolated island proves that "getting away" is always harder than it first seems. You never really know what troubles you're carrying until one rears up to eat you. Or, uh...*greet* you, I mean. Greet.

This next story is about a close personal friend of mine, and a long-time supporter of the *Planet Scumm* mission. Well, probably. I suppose Captain Starfall isn't exactly a "close" friend, but we did share a cell once. A cellblock, that is. We were definitely in the same prison megacomplex, for sure—one of the guards told me before I devoured him. Pedro Iniguez kicks open our airlock with the action-packed ***"Sierra Starfall and the Elders of the Spaceways."*** Sierra, if you're listening, we'd *love* to interview you on "*Planet Scumm.*" And I personally promise that we'd allow you and your crew to leave after the segment.

Continuing our long-running "*Transmission: Health*" series is Elena Sichrovsky, who comes to us with expert analysis on a dangerous new illness spreading through the 2nd Galactic Quadrant. I'm just getting the details on the threat now, but it looks like this illness... breaks down the skeletal system... liquifies internal organs...turns the afflicted into a quivering, melting puddle of goo... huh. Doesn't seem all that bad to be honest! But then again, I am not a doctor. Give *"Marigolds in Winter"* your attention, and decide for yourself!

We conclude with *"A Song for Ganymede,"* Austin P. Sheehan's investigative report on lobbying efforts for animal conservation within space communities. While many spacers seem willing to provide for such preserves, corporate interests have so far prevented full-scale adoption, and there are concerns that environmentalist groups may start to pursue extra-legal courses of action. I, for one, am all in for the greening of space habitats. Popping a domed city just hits different when you *know* you're wiping out an endangered species.

Stay tuned if you have the choice, folks! Spooky Scumm will be coming in after my shift for a few hours of *"The Galinstan Theatre on the Air."* After that, Spike E. Scumm will be in the command chair to wrangle our panel of celebrity "volunteers," who are having your donations beamed *directly* into their minds! All that and more on the Scumm Memorial Jellython!

PLANET SCUMM ISSUE #9

A BLOODY PULP

Spark & Fizz Books, 2020
Portland | Boston | New York

AUTHOR BIOS

HAILEY PIPER is a regular visitor to *Planet Scumm*. Her short fiction also appears in *Daily Science Fiction*, *The Arcanist*, *Flash Fiction Online*, and *Year's Best Hardcore Horror*. She's a member of the HWA and the author of numerous horror novellas. She lives with her wife in Maryland, but you can also find her at www.haileypiper.com or on Twitter via @HaileyPiperSays.

CLARISSA VAN DELL might be an eldritch abomination. She is especially fond of speculative fiction, mining her science education for oddities and irregularities that spark new story ideas. Her favorite things are loose leaf tea, the smell of rosewater, freshly grown mint, and vaccines. She loves cats and dogs equally, is not afraid of spiders, and aspires to be proficient in either archery or swordplay. Clarissa has both an Instagram and Facebook page (@clarissavandell) and is working on her debut YA novel, *Iceblade*.

PEDRO INIGUEZ lives in Eagle Rock, California, a quiet community in Northeast Los Angeles. He spends his time reading, writing, and painting, which stems from his childhood love of Science Fiction, Horror, and comic books. His work can be found in various magazines and anthologies such as: *Space and Time Magazine*, *Crossed Genres*, *Dig Two Graves*, *Writers of Mystery and Imagination*, *Deserts of Fire*, and *Altered States II*. His other works can be found on Amazon.

DAVID BUSBOOM is an Illinois-based writer with work appearing in such publications as *Shock Totem*, *Heroic Fantasy Short Stories*, *The Norwegian American*, and *The Saturday Evening Post*. His debut novella, "Nightbird," was published by Unnerving in 2018. More about him and his work can be found at davidbusboom.com.

ELENA SICHROVSKY is at the Shanghai University of Engineering Science and is also a longtime member of The Shanghai Writing Workshop. Her short stories have been published in *SciPhi Journal* and *Twenty-Two Twenty-Eight*, among others. Through her work, she seeks to find the beauty in the terrifying and the terror in the beautiful. She is also currently working on her first novel; you can follow her on Instagram @elenitasich for updates on her latest writing projects.

AUSTIN P. SHEEHAN is a writer of speculative fiction and a lover of language, literature and '90s TV. Armed with a psychology degree, he went out into the world to further study humanity, and now prefers the company of his wife and greyhounds. Although Austin wrote his debut novella while living in Melbourne's inner suburbs, you'll often find mountains in his stories, whether they are science fiction, fantasy, alternate history or horror. Find him on twitter @AustinPSheehan, or at www.austinpsheehan.com.

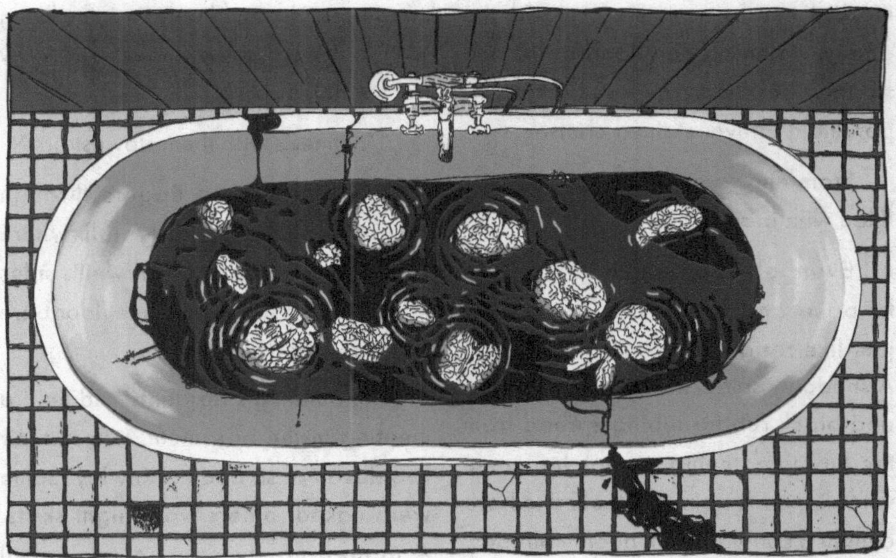

HAILEY PIPER

BRAIN TRUST

Never was there a worse invention than the telephone on a day off. Hans Jacobi almost didn't answer.

"You don't want Tommer alone here, Inspector," Constable Rogers said. "It's the Waisley case."

Mention of Waisley dragged Jacobi into the foggy evening, where lamplighters scurried between gaslights. Two constables stood watch outside a somber tenement building, its bricks reminding Jacobi of the toll this case had already taken.

"It was me who found it," Rogers said, leading Jacobi inside. "Passersby complained of the smell, and that's when I spotted the red dew on the stairs."

A thick trail, like strawberry jam, coated the steps inside. Up two flights, it crossed a single-room tenement's threshold, where Rogers had made his gruesome discovery.

"Like I always say, don your gloves when you handle organs." Jacobi plucked his own rubber mitts from his pocket as he spoke. No one lasted long in this work without a sense of morbid curiosity—or better still, morbid enthusiasm. He crossed the gooey, water-warped floorboards and stopped beside a clawfoot bathtub, its porcelain forever stained crimson.

From end to end, the bathtub was filled with brains.

Even gloved, he was hesitant to poke and prod. The strawberry jam-like residue coated wrinkly flesh. A shadowy spiderweb of copper pipes and black rubber tubing spread from the tub, threatening to snatch anyone who slipped too close. It looked to have caught a couple dozen people already.

"The materials are new," Jacobi said at last.

"Stuff that went missing from the factory," Rogers said. Went missing. Funny choice of words for how the factory workers had handed off supplies to strangers for reasons they couldn't remember, whose faces they hadn't seen.

"This is only a fraction of it. A test for whatever Waisley's colleagues are up to."

"Then they'll have the rest of the materials elsewhere."

"All the materials." Jacobi loomed over the tub, where the smell was a living thing. It wore the rot of human tissue, but also a disgusting medicinal sweetness. He could only imagine living with it. "Passersby complained? Why not the neighbors?"

"Tommer's with them downstairs."

Jacobi followed Rogers through a crack in the downstairs wall, where handprints painted the stairwell's sides in strawberry slime. The slate floor bore a deeper shade of red.

The building's residents had held a meeting in the basement, where their two dozen or so bodies now lay. Some were naked, others wore night skirts. A jagged cavity opened each skull where the brain should have been. Their fingers clutched kitchen knives and shards of glass as if driftwood at sea, post-shipwreck. To let go would bring true death. Their faces threw long shadows under the lantern light, dark screams made visible.

Inspector Tommer knelt at the edge of the slaughter. "They murdered each other. Every man for himself. And every woman."

Jacobi knelt beside him. "Waisley's colleagues made them do it. Like the factory workers."

Tommer snickered. "Suggesting mind control again?"

"People aren't birthday gifts you unwrap and empty. Someone made

BRAIN TRUST

them kill each other, and took what they needed—the brains. I suppose that makes you the safest man in town."

"You're mad as Waisley himself."

Jacobi didn't argue. The bodies did that for him. Disembodied brains were exciting, but he struggled to keep enthusiastic when the dead had faces. *Could've happened to you,* they said. Jacobi hoped he wouldn't have the dream again tonight. "I want another crack at him."

"Waisley's lost it." Tommer stood. He'd had enough death for tonight. "But I can arrange a meeting if you've time to waste."

"They have the other factory parts, and they've made two dozen people kill each other. They'll do it again. No, there isn't time to waste. Waisley knew them. The brains might jog his memory, make him tell us where to look."

That was the big question. Where? If Jacobi knew that, he could've ended this when Waisley's colleagues were only stealing machinery, not lives.

The lamplighters had finished their work when Jacobi walked home, a yellow-green glow that followed him from the house of death. He lit his apartment with candles to soften the night. The wicks cast warm, blobby shadows past his sparse furniture.

A smaller shadow walked in the door as he was settling down. Rosie threw a hand to her chest and gasped. "Papa, you scared me."

Jacobi rubbed his side as if he'd struck his hip on a countertop. He didn't want Rosie to see he'd been reaching for his pistol. "I scared you? You might be the scariest kid in town. Where were you?"

"With Mrs. Jenny. The old lady upstairs."

"Well, don't give the old man a heart attack." He hugged his daughter and stroked her hair, under which her skull and brain remained intact. "How about I fix dinner?"

While he chopped leeks and salted pork into a stew, Rosie rambled about her school friends, their little games and rumors, the world according to a seven-year-old. Some nights, her stories fogged together, an atmosphere Jacobi usually enjoyed without really noticing. Tonight, he hung on every word, as if her stories were the gallows.

He ladled the stew into two bowls and set them at the table, but didn't eat a bite until Rosie took her first mouthful. "My poison checker."

"Silly Papa." She flashed an approving smile as if she didn't notice the bland flavor, or even liked it.

"Will I be silly too when I grow up?"

"These defects tend to be hereditary. You might beat it. You can be anything when you grow up."

"I want to be an inspector, like you."

Jacobi slurped his stew quicker and didn't meet her eyes.

"What?" Her spoon clanked against the bowl. "Girls can do it. Girls are smart, too."

"That's the truth." Someday she was going to be smarter than him, he reasoned. Smart enough to realize she didn't need him anymore. She wouldn't be the first. "It's tough work."

"I can be tough."

"Is that so?" Jacobi tackled her from her seat, onto the floor. She struggled, laughing beneath his tickling hands. Their stew cooled on the table.

He lay awake on the sofa long after putting her to bed. The lit candle beside him that had once helped its fellows now sat alone, stretching the shadows tall and twisted. He was among Waisley's colleagues, five maniacs unseen since the Bragier accident. Unseen, except perhaps that one night when Jacobi crossed a strange cloaked man who dropped a bundle of copper pipes in an alleyway.

"Please, don't make me chase."

Jacobi had jogged over to the pipes.

The stranger hadn't looked back. He swept one arm at a brick wall as if he was splashing the surface of a pond. The bricks then splashed across Jacobi, who darted over the cobblestones to safety.

If there had been danger. When he returned at daybreak to hunt for clues, he found the wall intact. He never told anyone at the stationhouse. But, each day that a factory worker confessed to handing out supplies against his will, Jacobi wanted to say, "I understand."

And now two dozen people couldn't say the same. Jacobi had kitchen knives. What could Waisley's colleagues make him do?

If anything happened to him, he only had some small savings for Rosie to inherit. It was meant to grow, but she was growing instead, and feeding her cost more than it used to. Supposedly, she would get his pension, but who would advocate for its collection? Never hired a lawyer, never drew up a will. He knew the risks when he walked out the door, but Rosie? She never swore an oath to law and crown. If he didn't take care of these things while alive, no one was going to do it for him when he was gone.

The splashing wall haunted his dreams, but instead of raining bricks, it

BRAIN TRUST

rained brains. One of them belonged to Rosie, kept slipping out of his hands as he tried to snatch it, bring it home to her.

A lawyer would wait. These murderers needed catching.

The past was an inspector's best friend, yet time his nemesis. Every memory told possible answers, but as time passed those memories lost their tongues.

Jacobi visited the factory where machine parts had repeatedly been handed off to strangers. Workers and foremen had nothing new to tell. Deliveries meant for laboratories, the water treatment plant, the new locomotive—these thieves didn't care who they stole from.

"Where?" Jacobi had muttered the question a hundred times. The day was passing fast, every moment a fresh opportunity for Waisley's colleagues' next harvest.

Jacobi wasn't surprised to find himself where this whole mess had started. Bragier Research was once a proud institution for study into the workings and treatment of the mind. Today it was an acid-washed sinkhole twenty meters across. White residue showed where the chemical explosion had eaten through stone, soil, and flesh alike.

Waisley had assumed he was the only survivor until the first factory theft. He told the police that his colleagues were rebuilding, but what? He didn't know. The more he spoke, the harder the constables laughed.

No one laughed at that bathtub last night. Only Tommer was so thoughtless as to snicker in the basement among the dead. Where next would he lean over victims, brains stolen, and still think Waisley a madman?

Might as well re-check the tenement crime scene, home to the most recent clues.

The faint sun drooped to its late-afternoon height behind gray clouds, promises of a coming storm. It pulled the atmosphere taut across town. Whatever Waisley's colleagues were up to, they would do it tonight. Copper, rubber, and people, all their materials thrown toward some miserable purpose.

Where?

Tenement bricks screamed at Jacobi, threatened to dash his brain across cobblestones. Between those bricks, past the window where a bathtub full of brains lingered, a shadow crossed the glass. Jacobi slipped inside, pistol ready, up the steps still sticky with slime. At the tub, a dark-cloaked stranger's steel tongs groped one brain, turned it over, set it down, and tried another. Water-warped wood creaked under his shoes as he turned to Jacobi.

"Afternoon, Inspector," Waisley said, his face pale and gaunt. He hadn't seen the sun in some time. "Figured you'd be back. You wanted to speak?"

Jacobi holstered his pistol. "We might've met someplace nicer."

"This room reminds me of Bragier." Waisley's tongs rotated the drooling brain. "Our research was chemical. I never knew they needed organs, especially not human. It was no trouble for them, I can tell. Removing a brain is simple once you're past the skull. Almost like it wants to be removed."

"But what for?"

"Maybe to connect with us again. They can't speak anymore. All communication flows between minds. When they try this mental speech with us, we only see things." Waisley pointed his tongs at Jacobi. "A trick they swiftly weaponized."

Soft rain struck the roof above. Jacobi thought of bricks. "And that's how they controlled the factory workers? The people downstairs?"

"It isn't direct control. More like a psychic attack. Their minds assault yours, trying to get their way, but the effect manifests differently for everyone. For them, it's like shouting, but I saw my field surgeon days. We don't cross paths now. One memory is enough."

Jacobi took him by the shoulder. "We need to know where they are. We can stop them if we know."

"They're everywhere, Inspector. They're more than five men now, their minds have reached so far. They manipulate this town from hidden places. Soon they'll emerge, and this tub says they won't be alone. The mind is the key to a door only they can see." Waisley let the brain slither out of his tongs.

"What will it open for them? Imagine, a world of pure mind, like living in a dream. Are we the key, the door, the—"

The tongs slipped from his hands and clattered against copper pipes. He dropped screaming into a ball, his cloak seeping into red slime.

Jacobi knelt and shook his shoulder. "Doctor?"

"Don't make me take his leg!" Waisley shouted. "I can't bear the blood anymore!"

Something scrambled from the doorway. Jacobi followed, down the stairs and out the building door, where a stranger in a rain-spotted cloak loped across the street, head hidden under a bulging hood. Jacobi went for his gun.

"Inspector!" Constable Rogers appeared so quick that Jacobi almost shot him. "It's only me."

The figure was now a distant blot. "We need to call the stationhouse and rally horsemen," Jacobi said.

"Inspector, there's already been a call." Rogers leaned close. "It's your daughter."

Rosie. Jacobi pushed past Rogers and followed the trail of unlit gaslights. He hadn't told Rogers to help Waisley—didn't matter. Rosie needed him. Rain spattered his hair, his coat. Mud slurped at his boots where cobbles had gone missing outside his apartment building.

How had Rogers known he'd be at the tenement building? Even Waisley had only hazarded a guess they might meet there. His words rang in Jacobi's head. *Their minds assault yours, trying to get their way.*

Or to get away.

Jacobi slowed at his building doorway. Waisley's colleagues thought they were funny, did they? Thunder laughed across the sky. Jacobi sneered at the darkening clouds and started up the stairs. They could have done worse, turned him into a brainless corpse. They

could have actually taken Rosie.

His boot made a squelching sound as he reached his floor. Red slime pooled underfoot.

No, not here. He would take being fooled a thousand times. He hurried to his apartment, keys jangling in trembling hands. His free hand grasped his pistol.

"Rosie?"

The apartment lay frozen under the storm's gray hue. Nothing moved across its cold floorboards.

"Rosie, answer me."

Up the stairs, Jacobi pounded on Mrs. Jenny's door. No answer. He punched other doors, only throwing echoes through apathetic hallways. No one was home, the building hollowed out.

Waisley's colleagues had been collecting materials.

Jacobi returned to his apartment and rang the stationhouse. He would have to organize a manhunt, rally volunteers, and hope they were of stronger minds than his, so that Waisley's colleagues wouldn't set them against each other. Psychic attacks, stolen brains. What defense could they have?

Perhaps if someone had no brain. Tommer's voice was tinny in the earpiece. "What are you on about?

We're readying to end this."

Jacobi's fist squeezed the cool metal. "You know where they are?"

Tommer chuckled. "Not so smart now, are you? They're back at Bragier, gathered in the pit. We'll see you in the morning, Jacobi."

"I visited the sinkhole this afternoon. There's nothing."

The line went dead. Jacobi called again, no answer, and threw the jangly phone at the wall. Tommer was a fool, but he couldn't fool the entire police force. Someone had put slimy hands in the stationhouse.

Jacobi would have to save Rosie on his own. His gaze traced his floorboards as if peering at a town map.

"Figure it out, man. Save her."

Waisley's colleagues were clever, but they weren't perfect. Pipes. Tubes. Brains. Location. The tenement had been a testing ground with a fraction of what they needed, but it wasn't right. Not enough people, not enough space. What was he missing? The floorboards crawled closer, mixing with the shadows cast by lightning.

Thunder rattled the windows. Slanting, watery sheets lapped at the glass, distorting the faint green gaslights as they sparked to life down the street.

The town was only a warped smear of soggy gray shapes.

The wooden tenement floor had been soaked and dried. Fluid had pumped through pipes, but the red residue Waisley's colleagues left in their wake didn't dry. It stayed. The brains might have been submerged in the tub.

No one had considered yet another material. It had been too simple.

Jacobi charged back to the street. The storm drenched him, pulled cobbles loose to throw mud and puddles in his path, snatched at him with gusty fingers. He never slowed.

Only one place in town held a vast supply of water—the water treatment plant. Waisley's colleagues might have holed up there since before the factory thefts, at first contented with its copper pipes, but then needing more. How far back had they known they needed brains? Since Bragier fell?

The water treatment plant's boxy silhouette loomed black against the flicker of lightning. Gaslights only glowed so close, and then stood dark outside the entrance. No one had bothered to lock the front gate. Jacobi pushed through the steel doors into a lengthy hall, its edges burdened with grime.

One dark cloak slipped through a door at the far end. A straggler suggested they hadn't started yet. Whoever they had in there might still keep their brains. Waisley's colleagues couldn't have Rosie's.

Jacobi stuck his head through the door. It was worse than expected.

Maybe thirty people lived in his apartment building. Over a hundred crowded the steel floor before a foreboding pool. Addle-minded, they didn't notice Jacobi. Most were grown, but between their shuffling legs he spotted children in woolen dresses. Copper pipes crisscrossed above their heads and fed black tubes into the water.

Waisley's colleagues gathered on a platform at the center of the pool, connected to the main floor by a railed bridge. Dark robes hid most of their hunched figures. From their sleeves grew bony, yellow-gray fingers that curled and uncurled. Their faces were bony, too, the skin hugged tight around lipless teeth and missing noses, seared and blanched in Bragier's awful chemicals.

The caps of their skulls were gone. Each one's brain had outgrown its cradle through the scalp and eye sockets. Their heads were more brains than faces and features.

Jacobi crept onto the steel floor. "Rosie?" he whispered.

An invisible fist squeezed the crowd; those closest to the bridge picked things off the floor and turned to each other. Glass shards gleamed between their fingers, already drawing blood. An elderly woman plunged her shard into a younger man's neck. The rest of the crowd at the pool's edge followed her example, jabbing each other anywhere but those precious brains. Only they could say what dreams they saw.

Jacobi's heart clambered up his throat. "Rosie!"

"Papa?"

Between the sleepwalkers' legs, a small round-faced shadow emerged on hands and knees. She didn't look hurt, only wide-eyed, her lip quivering.

"Papa, help!"

He was supposed to help everyone, an oath sworn to law and crown. No more bathtubs full of brains.

His fingers latched around Rosie's wrist, and they ran. Gurgling screams chased them down the long hall, through the steel doors, past the creaking gate of the water treatment plant, into the splattering rain. No one followed down the dark street, human or otherwise.

He would try the stationhouse again. Someone else would be here soon. Even if too late to stop the slaughter, Waisley's colleagues would go to prison or a laboratory, wherever they belonged. Gaslights offered paths to familiar places. Lightning's brilliance humbled their glow, and Jacobi turned to watch it fork toward the plant. If only it would strike the creatures, end this by act of heaven, and ease his conscience.

His hand was empty. Rosie had separated from him.

"Rosie?" He darted back toward the plant. Waisley's colleagues must have put her under psychic attack again, led her back to the pool. "Rosie, call to me!"

Mud had displaced cobblestones from beneath the lit gaslights, a sloppy trail that slipped into the plant's shadow. Rainfall pooled in Jacobi's footprints. There were no others beside his.

It isn't direct control. More like a psychic attack.

She had been running with him. The splashing bricks had fooled him, and Rogers outside earlier, but nothing else.

Their minds assault yours, trying to get their way.

He'd only been on this case a few weeks; Rosie was seven years old. The Rosie he'd pulled from the plant? She was the fake. The real Rosie was still in there, about to die. Rosie, his poison checker, always coming home right behind him. The reason he didn't want to leave.

But the effect manifests differently for everyone.

He stumbled between cobbles, retracing his muddy footprints. Memories orbited, his mind snatching at them, but they were untouchable starlight, only echoes of a presence. Who was Rosie's mother? What had she looked like? His mind hadn't put enough effort into the manifestation.

He passed from the lit gaslights and under cover of the dark ones outside the water treatment plant. Thunder laughed at him again.

Waisley's colleagues had already cracked skulls open and were sliding their prizes gently into the water. They had set their crowd to killing each other in waves. Methodical, patient slaughter. Jacobi didn't count the dead. They were fewer than the living—that had to be good enough.

Between the doorway and the crowd, Rosie turned bright eyes to him. She was supposed to grow up smarter than him, someday realize she didn't need him anymore, but hopefully stay anyway.

He hugged her, stroked her hair. She felt real. He couldn't remember if she smelled like she should. Copper scents and tastes overwhelmed his senses. When he stood, he held her against his side. Just in case. His free hand drew his pistol and aimed over the crowd.

"Papa?"

The shot pounded hard through the metal room, shocking the crowd into ducking. Waisley's colleagues had their hands too full to react fast. One head exploded across dark robes, red slime bursting from the sagging brain. Another bullet threw a second creature to the floor.

Rosie clawed at Jacobi's coat. "Papa, don't!"

Waisley's colleagues would regain control of the situation given even one spare second. Jacobi's next bullet hit a shoulder, and the next hit a head.

The room contorted around him, its shadows sliding slender claws into his skull. Two creatures remained. He concentrated on them, their horrible skulls, and hoped they couldn't twist bullets. His last two shots ate t hrough their seared faces.

"Stop, Papa!"

He lowered his gun and strode through teeming sleepwalkers toward the pool. They were coming awake around him, an uncertain, screaming river that flowed toward the exit hallway. He shouldered around them, over dead bodies, some with untouched skulls, others now crimson bowls that leaked into the town's water supply.

Waisley's fallen colleagues lay on the platform, all dead except one. The bullet had ripped across his cheek, grazed his brain, but not put him down for good. Jacobi opened his pistol, let fall the casings, and slid fresh shells into its chambers.

Rosie sprang from his side and

hunkered over the last creature's misshapen head. "Why, Papa? They just wanted to escape the loud world. Why couldn't you let them?"

The pistol trembled in Jacobi's fingers. He could slip his finger from the trigger guard, holster the pistol, and leave this place with Rosie in hand. Neither had to look back. It could be so easy.

Except if he strayed too far from Waisley's last colleague, he would stray empty-handed.

His finger squeezed the trigger. The blast rocketed through Rosie and smattered the creature's overripe brain across the wet platform. When Jacobi blinked, Rosie was gone.

Human remains bobbed around the island of inhuman corpses. Blood, drinking water, and red slime stewed together in the calm pool. Thunder banged overhead, but it no longer sounded like laughter, maybe never had. Jacobi could divide memory and fantasy no more than he could separate the fluids that surrounded him. It was like fighting a dream of falling bricks, miserable yet never wanting to awaken.

But someday, the dreams must die.

   BRAIN TRUST

DAVID BUSBOOM

AHEAD OF DRAGONS

I've been trailing Doc Hausen for nearly a month. According to the information from Uncle Linnie, he's built something in Utah that'll bring a whole swarm of dragons down on his head. Good thing they can only read *each other's* minds.

He's headed east and laying low. I miss him by about five hours in Chicago and spend the morning going around to all the ticket officers, getting chummy with agents. Finally find out Hausen bought a ticket to Champaign, Illinois, so I fan on down there and cool. No dragon city hovering over this county.

I spot Hausen in the third joint I check. He matches Uncle Linnie's photo: big man with a round, cheery face and smooth skin, very pink in person. His mouth is loose and wet and his eyes are light blue. I think his eyes are the smallest I've ever seen.

He's kept the nature of his invention pretty close to his vest, but luck is the only thing that's kept him alive. He looks scared, drinking lemonade with an electro-sword on his belt like a fat-handled *wakizashi*.

"Excuse me," I say, extending a hand.

"Dian Fox. Haven't I seen you around Linnie Turtledove's in Philly?"

Uncle Linnie practically founded the Underground.

"Maybe," he says, smiling. "What do you drink?"

"Whiskey."

"Are you even old enough?"

"Twenty-one last week."

Hausen waves to the bartender. "Whiskey for the lady." He looks at me. "Have you been in town long?"

"I've just come down from Chi to check things out," I say. "Things don't look so hot. I'll probably go back to Philly tomorrow, should you need a traveling companion."

"How is it you know Mr. Turtledove?"

"He and Dad flew in the Great War. The one against the Germans, that is."

"Ah," Hausen says, small eyes blinking, round head bobbing in a slow nod. "That was a hard time for me here."

Too late I remember the origin of his name, catch his faint accent.

"I'm sorry," I blurt. "I meant no offense."

He holds up an understanding hand.

"You weren't even born," he says, sighing. "Who'd ever have thought I'd long for those days back? Ignorant patriots are much easier to ignore than monsters from beyond the clouds."

I buy him more lemonade and have my whiskey and we talk about Philly. I register myself with him as one of the boys, so to speak, and find out he's taken a room at the Francis Hotel. I take a pedicab over to do the same, flip the register back a day or so and find Hausen's name to make sure, then go up and wash and lay down to smoke a cigarette and figure out the details.

According to Uncle Linnie, whatever Hausen's built is a weapon, one that could really help the Underground even the odds a bit. I can't be sure of that, but it's enough. The point is to get him to Philly, and into one of the two or three places he'll be safe.

◆

I must sleep a couple of hours, because it's dark when I wake up. Somebody's knocking at the door. I get up and stumble over, switch on the light, and open it. It's Hausen, electro-sword and all. I mumble something about coming in and sitting down, and go over to the sink to splash cold water on my face.

When I turn around he's sitting on the bed looking scared. I offer him a cigarette and he takes it with a shaking hand.

"Sorry I woke you up like that," he says.

"S'all right."

He leans forward. "I've got to get out of here—right away," he says in a low voice. "I want to know how much it's worth to you to help me out of Champaign tonight."

The man's more scared than I thought.

"Sure," I say, sort of hesitantly.

"Listen," he says. "I got here Saturday morning. I was going to stay here long enough to lay low, and then move on. The dragons have been on my tail twelve days, at least. They're here. When I got back to the hotel a little while ago they were outside. They came in late this afternoon. I changed rooms as quietly as possible."

He's silent so long that I laugh a little. "So what?"

"I've got to duck, quick," he goes on. "There're two of them. They've been walking around. You said you were going back to Philly. I saw your name on the register when I came in, and remembered your offer to take me along."

I check my watch. Not quite nine o'clock.

"There isn't a train till midnight."

"Can't we rent a tandem freight bike?"

"Train's faster. And safer."

He pulls the biggest roll I've ever seen out of his pocket and skims off a couple bills. "If it's a question of money...."

I shake my head with what I hope is a suggestion of dignity.

"Maybe we can get a bike tonight." I get up and put on my oversized coat. "How about your stuff?"

"I have to sneak up to my room to get it," he says. "I'll meet you down-stairs. I've already paid my bill."

I go downstairs and check out. The clerk behind the counter is a big blond kid with glasses.

One of the dragons stands outside, just a few yards from the lobby entrance. It's about nine feet tall, nude save the antigrav device belted around its waist. It doesn't seem to notice me through the glass, but then it's hard to tell with those faceted eyes. I get as close to the stairwell as I can and lean against the wall, waiting as modestly as possible.

This whole layout looks bad. What's taking Hausen so long? Where's the other dragon?

After about five more seconds I start getting nervous. As I open the door to the stairwell there's a crash and a scream close together, someplace upstairs. The dragon seems as startled as me; it unfurls its full twenty-foot wingspan, and takes off. Probably communicating with its partner, the way they do—or at least trying to.

I can take trouble or leave it alone, only I always take it. Like a sap, I go upstairs, two or three at a time. The blond clerk is close behind me.

There's a man in a long, woolly bathrobe standing in the corridor on the third floor, and he points to a door. We go in. Hausen's lying face down in a pool of blood in the middle of the room. Beyond him, close to the wall, is the large body of a dragon, also face down, long tail and limbs still seizing. The big window is shattered inward.

The clerk turns a beautiful shade of green and stands there, staring at the dragon. I roll Hausen over on his back, getting his blood on my boots. There's a deep slash in his side, under the arm. He's dead.

The dragon's a little smaller than its partner outside, but that's not saying much. A curved, fourteen-inch fighting claw extends from one heel, covered in blood. Its huge wings are half-spread over most of the body, but just under the base of one I can see the bloody tip of Hausen's electro-sword protruding from its leathery back. The dragon's blood is darker than Hausen's.

The man in the shaggy bathrobe peeks in and then hurries across the hall and into another room. I hear him yell the news to somebody there.

I tap the clerk on the shoulder and point at Hausen. The clerk swallows a couple of times.

"He's dead," he says, and looks back at the dragon, hypnotized by its weakening convulsions.

AHEAD OF DRAGONS

Then about two dozen people come into the room all at once.

The sheriff was in a pool hall across the street. He looks at Hausen, then at the clerk, then at me, and finally scratches his head and goes over to look at the dragon, careful not to touch. It's now barely twitching.

The dragon must've surprised Hausen in his room while he was getting his things and spurred him, probably wanting what we did. His stuff's all still here. The sheriff and a couple of deputies search everything.

All they find on Hausen is the roll he flashed on me—seventy-two hundred-dollar bills tucked into his pants pocket—and the usual keys, cigarettes, and whatnot. No letters or papers of any kind. There's one big suitcase in his room, and inside, concealed under dirty clothes, is a miniature version of a dragon's antigravity belt, affixed with some additional controls, two small nozzles, and a fuel tank.

"It's a jetpack!" the clerk says.

"A jetpack?" says the sheriff.

But it is. An honest-to-God jetpack, just like from the Buck Rogers comic strips I used to read with Dad, before the sky ripped open over California.

"In a half-hour or so the dragons will descend on this place and tear it apart, for revenge and for this gadget," I say. "It'll be a cinch for them. I've got to take this out of here."

"You?" the sheriff says.

I open my jacket, let him see Dad's M1911 holstered beneath. Firearms of any kind are rare as cars now, thanks to the dragons. The old service pistol is my badge.

The sheriff understands, lets me grab the roll of cash and the jetpack—it's a lot lighter than it looks. He helps me fasten the bulky thing around my waist, under my loose jacket. "Get out," he says, when it's done. "Do you have a bike?"

"No."

"Take mine." He hands me the key. "The black police bike locked across the street."

I screw down the back stairway and out the side door. I have to figure this out myself now. They have a complicated enough mess on their hands, and if I ride hard I can make it to Philly in four days or so.

Riding away from the hotel it looks like everybody in town is on the way there. What'll they do when the dragons return? I don't stay to find out, immediately starting east out of Champaign. Nothing chases me, and within the hour

I'm following a discreet country road through a light drizzle.

I bend forward over the handlebars, my eyes moving regularly from the glistening road ahead to the small rearview mirror and back. I pedal steadily, pacing myself. There's no sound but the roar of the wind and the singing of the tires. They screech on the wet pavement as I round a large, shallow curve.

My headlight catches a dragon standing squarely in the road.

I swerve, skid halfway across the road, jam on the brakes, jerk the handlebars hard over. The bike goes by the dragon at nine miles an hour, jostles over the gravel at the road's shoulder and comes to a stop with a blown tire. I barely manage to keep from crashing. The dragon disappears into the darkness, but I know it's still there. It spurred the tire on purpose.

I ditch the bike and look for the dragon; it might be the one from the hotel parking lot, but there's no way to be sure. I reach into my jacket and draw Dad's pistol—no use hiding now; with those feline ears and sensitive bug-eyes it'll have a much easier time detecting me than I it.

I hear the sound of wings approaching and open up with the gun. The dragon comes down almost on top of me, bleeding from the chest and leg but still conscious and flapping, short beak open in a silent roar. I put two more bullets in its five-lobed brain and it stops kicking. The only sounds are the light rain and my own heavy breathing.

There are more coming. I don't have any options. I holster the gun and throw off my jacket. I can't help but laugh at what I'm considering.

Then I think of Hausen, fighting to the death to defend this thing, traveling halfway across the country to ensure it got into the proper hands. My hands.

I don't know how to use it, but maybe I can figure it out well enough to get to the next town. Trying to proceed on foot would be suicide.

I hear at least three pairs of wings flapping in the dark distance. They're already here.

I run east along the road, away from the wings, pressing buttons as I go, feeling like an avenger from the 25th century.

The nozzles fire. It's as if a great, trembling hand is dragging me up. My back and legs are hot.

I'm flying.

The wings are close enough now that I can hear them over the jetpack. I draw Dad's pistol, almost crashing

     AHEAD OF DRAGONS

in the process, and fire blindly into my wake. One set of wingbeats grows frantic, then stops. The others continue, steady behind me. I keep firing, but they've moved out of the way. They're getting closer.

I drop the gun. It's spent anyway.

They're going to catch me.

Maybe they'll take me to one of their cities. The one over Chicago. Maybe they'll just kill me, destroy the jetpack like they did all man-made aircraft.

But I don't want to think about that. They haven't caught me yet, and right now I just want to think about how it feels to fly ahead of dragons. I bet it's how Dad felt in his biplane, back in '32.

Alive.

CLARISSA VAN DELL

ON THE ORIGIN OF FEAR

I remember the day my boat washed up on the island, after I deserted the *Crescent Moon*. I had grown to hate sailing, and my position as the man who maintained the Moon's ship-shape status. The mainland featured in my dreams nightly, and our short stays at port were hardly enough time to savor the feel of earth underfoot. After being offshore for over a year, the sun seemed to cast a permanent glare on the ocean.

One night, after the rest of the crew-members drank themselves to sleep, I packed. I didn't take much: some food and water, a gun, and my extra clothes.

It was time I found a bar and ordered the strongest drink they had, I figured. I left the sleeping quarters and had just stepped onto the deck when a hulking silhouette approached.

"Boy," he said. I could feel the hairs on the back of my neck stiffen. "So, you're leaving at last."

I dared to lift my head toward him, just able to make out his face in the moonlight. The captain stood before me, one eye completely clouded over in gray. A formidable man of seventy, condescending and sharp-tongued.

He seemed to enjoy treating me like a child, and was one of the reasons I grew to detest sailing. "You expected me to leave?"

Scoffing, he took hold of my chin. His hand was like ice. "I expected you to leave since the day you set foot on this ship. I've seen your kind before, boy, more interested in book-reading than an honest day's work. Thinking you're smart. I bet you haven't even figured out where you're going."

"I'm not a boy. I'm almost twenty."

He ignored me. "You may know a thing or two, but that thinking's gonna get you killed someday. Reading things that don't matter to the real world, getting uppity with your superiors. I can hire any man to take your place. I couldn't give a damn what happens to you." He finally let go of me. "Tangiers is about an hour due east. That ought to be civil enough for you."

I blinked, not sure how to take his words. "Thank you, sir?"

"You're rowing there. I'm not about to divert from course for the likes of you." His good eye peered into my soul one last time. "You read a thousand books, you think you're some sort of special, but you're as stupid as every lad who's fancied himself a man. Let me give you a tip." He started walking away, one hand on his belt. "Get off this ship, and pray to God you never see me again, 'less I shoot you. I've had enough of your mouthing, but I can't let deserters get away scot-free."

He disappeared from view, and I hurried toward the wooden lifeboats to stow my belongings inside. The captain terrified me, yet for once I was grateful for his command. Rowing for an hour would be an arduous task, but one that I thought possible on a calm night, with the full moon above.

I rowed that night for half the hour, or longer. I remember seeing lights, shining afar from the African port. I also remember my weak flesh beginning to cave to a seductive lullaby that came from the waves, lapping against the outside of my vessel...

◆

I opened my eyes to the sun and realized that the familiar bobbing of the ocean was gone. Everything was still. Too still. I sat up straight and found the boat stationary... I smiled, though I still had no idea where I was. The only clues I had were this new strip of beach and the jungle forest that sat inland, opposite the glare of the ocean. Just those, and the eerie silence.

There was nothing to suggest the island was inhabited. I don't mean just human inhabitants; there weren't any animal noises, at all. Unease settled in my stomach, and I reached for my gun, thankful that it remained untouched by the sea. It was a smart metal pistol that I had only used twice before. Once for self-defense, and once more as a result of my temper running away from me.

Where to go? What to do? Could I escape, or at least stay alive until someone found me here? I clutched the precious thing to my chest, running my hand along the barrel, deep in thought. Then, I heard the sound of soft breathing behind me.

I turned and aimed my pistol, arm shaking, at the monstrosity that was watching me. Her head was oversized on her spindly body, with long arms ending with hands a third the size of mine. Her bare torso was so thin, I could have grabbed her and broken her back upon my knee. For clothes, she wore only a large, colorful headdress and long grass skirt. That didn't matter. No, she reminded me more of a broomstick than a woman. I would have Darwin explain that to me, if he could!

I kept the gun on her for a full minute. Then I realized that her eyes, big, black, and watery, were aimed at the gun not in fear, but curiosity. I put it down carefully and she followed it until I had the gun hidden in the boat, then she returned her gaze to me. With only a small rustling noise from her grass skirt, she seemed to float over to me. "Ah, hello?"

She didn't respond. Not right away. She smiled, though, which still looked grotesque on that strange head of hers. "Do you live here, miss?" I asked, though the obvious answer was yes. She was still smiling. Before I came up with another question to ask, she was pulling at my hand, urging me to get out of the boat. I stood and let her lead me into the jungle.

Back then, the jungle was lush. It was green, filled with flowers and fruits of every sort and hue. And the butterflies! Every direction I looked, five or more butterflies perched on the flowers or leaves, their wings as big as my hand! But the most wonderful thing of all? How accessible everything was. Paths wound their way through the greenery, allowing one to pick whatever fruit they pleased. No one maintained the foliage to make it so; it was as if the entire jungle grew to be as convenient as possible. With her giant petal headdress, the waif guiding me seemed to belong to that jungle.

Finally, I could see sunlight past a row of trees. My guide let go of my arm and dashed for the warm light, into some sort of valley. I raced after

ON THE ORIGIN OF FEAR

her; she was graceful as a deer. As soon as I broke through the final row of trees, I saw their village nestled in the center of the island. Crowds of creatures wore those petal crowns atop their bulbous heads. They lived in large huts of grass, made unique with flower—like birds' nests, almost.

I noticed that five or six different headdresses were moving in my direction. My first reaction was to go for my pistol. But no, I had left that in the boat, like the idiot boy I was. Still, if it came down to a fight, I was definitely stronger than any one of their twig-like bodies. I decided to meet them halfway, and started out into the sunlight.

I was only about a quarter of the way to their village before we met. We stopped about a foot from each other; they had no concept of personal space, it seemed. We stood in silence for several seconds, then one of them— the first creature I met at the beach— reached for my jaw and tugged at it. I batted her hand away. "Ow."

They all came closer, and I grew uncomfortable. "Is there something I can help you with?"

Their eyes widened with that. They turned to each other and started to wave their arms, flapping their hands. That's when I realized that speaking, for these people, was not a concept.

"Uh, well, it was nice to meet you, but I—" They grabbed my clothes, four of them at once. I could have forced them off, but their grips were gentle. They couldn't have grasped my arm, as it was too thick and wide for their miniscule hands. I allowed them to tug at my clothing and let them lead me to their village.

◆

They were kind, if a tad peculiar. Though they never spoke, they had a way of somehow knowing whatever I needed. With them, I was never scared. They introduced me to all the food sources on the island and prepared a bed for me in the largest hut available. No chief, tribal leader, or council led them; instead, they all wandered around the village without any argument or disharmony.

The most communication I saw from them was the occasional hand gesture that I couldn't quite follow, or maybe the slow blinks and serene smiles they'd exchange. I never gave much thought to science before reaching the island, but the flower people fascinated me. If only I were a biologist; if I ever made it back to civilization, I'd never have to work a day in my life again!

I didn't just take things from them,

oh no. Not the flower people, whose kindness and sincerity rivaled that of the angels. No, I helped them gather food. My strength was at least tenfold theirs, and the nuts and fruits seemed to fall off branches with only the touch of my hand.

That was my other major discovery. The island had sentience, or something akin to it. Every fruit was sweet and delicious, every tree easy to climb. Sometimes I thought I heard laughter when the wind rushed past my face. Despite being stranded on this uncharted island, I never pined for the home I'd left behind. This island was my home. It grew used to my presence, and accepted me as one of its own.

❧

Maybe a few weeks passed. One afternoon, I was lounging on my "bed"—a simple pallet of leaves and flower petals—when Flower Girl from the beach entered, eyes wide. I lifted my head toward her, curious about what it was she wanted. "Yes, did you want me?" I asked. Though they didn't understand my words, the flower people seemed to get a kick out of hearing the noises that came from my mouth.

Though she gave a small smile, she still seemed alarmed. No, these people knew no fear or alarm. Excitement, yes.

She walked over to me and tugged at my shirt, which I'd torn sleeveless after giving in to the heat. I learned days ago that meant she wanted me to follow her. "All right, all right, I'll go with you," I said, getting to my feet. She didn't let go, but led me out the door of the hut, through the village and out into the surrounding jungle.

At first it didn't surprise me. The flower people often went on excursions to the jungle to gather food, though they didn't seem to like leaving their sunny clearing for too long. To my surprise, as I followed her, the trees grew taller, and the canopy began to obscure the blue sky altogether. When we reached what I knew to be the heart of the jungle, my eyebrows rose, and I halted. "Where are you taking me?"

She continued to pull at my shirt, though she was straining as much as she could, without any success at moving me forward. Realizing her efforts were futile, she turned to look at me with wonder. I don't know if they believed in gods, but if they did, I'm certain she thought me one. She continued to stare at me, the immovable being, for a few seconds, then tugged at my shirt again. I realized she wasn't going to give me any answers, no matter how often I asked, so I allowed her to lead me once more.

　　ON THE ORIGIN OF FEAR

We emerged from the jungle onto the beach.

"Now what?" I asked Flower Girl. She continued leading me across the sand, until we arrived at the lifeboat which brought me here. "My boat?"

She finally let go of me, and I watched as she approached it—without fear, as usual. She reached inside with one wiry arm, and retrieved a small bundle wrapped in brown paper. I recognized it; I took it with me from the *Crescent Moon* that fateful night.

I took it as soon as she held it out to me and peeled the paper away to expose four or five sticks of salted beef. The aroma hit my nostrils, and I slid one of the sticks from its paper envelope and into my mouth. It was heavenly; there weren't any animals on the island except for those large butterflies that flitted everywhere in the jungle. "Mmmm." A single-note hum buzzed in my back teeth.

Flower Girl stared at me. Again, she wasn't afraid, but rather curious. I stared back at her and watched as she took a stick of beef from the package and copied the way I jabbed the end into my mouth. It was funny the way she did it, like a boy working up the nerve to let a lit cigar touch his lips. Her eyes went wide as the taste registered.

"Good?" I asked, after swallowing my own mouthful. "Never had beef before, have you?"

I didn't know how I expected her to react. Probably not at all. It wasn't as if she knew what I was saying, anyway. "Mmmm," she hummed. "Mmmm! Mmmmmmm!"

I couldn't help but feel unnerved as her eyes grew wider and, for the first time, took on a look of hunger. She wanted more.

◆

I was reassured by the fact that my caretakers did have the capacity for speech; I could teach them to be civilized. Well, not all of them. There were two distinct sorts of flower people, those who hummed and those who did not.

Those who didn't hum walked past me, as if I were another flower. But the other ones... Where first I had been the only source of noise in the village, soon choruses of hums rose up from roads, houses, the jungle. It put me at ease, and I began to think of the flower people as my friends, rather than the grotesque monsters I first saw.

The "hummers" were also the ones who came to me for meat. At first I had no clue how to help them, as there were no animals on the island. Yet, I came to a solution: I took my little vessel out a few yards, and managed to net a few fish. These I cooked over a fire (the villagers had never seen fire before—another gift I brought to them). I then carved off pieces to hand out to the young villagers. Most accepted with relish, but Flower Girl seemed unsatisfied. I wasn't surprised, as the delights of fish fail to deliver after sampling beef.

It was soon after that things got strange, though I was too blind to see it. I was cooking a pair of fish over my driftwood fire on the beach, when I felt the hummers circle around. "Hold on a second. I still have to—" One of those little hands tapped on my shoulder.

I turned away from the flames and fish to see the whole lot of them grinning, holding a grass-woven basket of shredded meat. I took a chance and dipped my hand in that mess of flesh and blood. I had no clue what it was; they skinned it well, presumably copying the way I sliced the scales from the fish.

There must be some kind of animal on the island that I hadn't seen, I thought. I was a bumbling foreigner in this forest, and my new friends seemed to be descendants of the trees. There was no reason any animal should expect me to let it live in peace.

"Excellent job!" I said, even though my praise was lost on them—or maybe not, seeing the way their eyes and grins widened. I roasted the small pieces up for them in minutes, and they all enjoyed real meat at last.

It was an odd taste, to be honest. Meat, but with a fibrous quality to it. I only managed to eat half before I couldn't stand it anymore. One of the flower people was glad to finish my share, and I couldn't help but feel a surge of pride. They devoured it, piece by piece, until the evening was beginning to color the sky dark.

"Well, you know where to find me tomorrow."

They all gave that hum, almost as if they understood what I meant. They departed one by one after that, leaving me to sit by my small fire and reflect on the weeks I had spent on this island. The flower people were strange, but kind and charitable. And I was helping them in return, by teaching them the wonders of cooked meat and how to speak. It was a pleasant feeling. It didn't last long.

The sun set by the time I started back to the village, and deep violet stretched overhead. That was when I started to notice the grass wrapping around my legs, turning a simple trek through the jungle into a struggle. I'm sure I got

ON THE ORIGIN OF FEAR

turned around a few times in attempting to make my way through the wilderness into the clearing as a result. It's the only way to explain how I found it.

Lightning crackled through the violet night, revealing a pair of obsidian eyes between my raised foot and the ground. Thunder echoed overhead, drowning out my surprised yelp. I found myself on the ground, three feet back from the flower person's head that lay before me. A full five minutes passed before my heart settled, and I managed to examine the large mass before me. It wore no headdress, leaving one smooth scalp and an agape mouth. Again, its final expression was not of fear, but something else—simple surprise. Maybe that expression was why the whole thing was so disturbing, and why I ended up vomiting in the grass.

Once my stomach was empty, I examined the rest of the body. I assured myself that it must have been natural causes. An infection, or a bad fall, or poisonous fruit. There wasn't even any indication that it was the source of...dinner. I was overreacting. I told myself that until I almost believed it, then I moved the grass aside from the base of the head.

The good thing was that the body was still attached. The bad thing was that the flesh was completely stripped from the bone, the organs resting in a neat pile within the rib cage. I dry-heaved for the next few minutes.

This was bad. This was very bad. And it was my fault. Still, there was no sign of foul play, which was good. *Cannibals were tolerable, as long as the food died on its own, right?* Justification after justification, none of them easing the tumor of guilt and horror growing in my stomach. But what chewed at me most was that these kind, sensitive beings could commit such a sin against their own kind. Was this my doing? If so, could God ever forgive me?

◆

The next day, they brought me more meat. I cooked it at their wordless insistence, but I never placed any of it into my mouth. Fish was suitable enough for me. The next few days were the same, forcing me to conclude that the worst-case scenario was also reality. They were "hunting" their own. The very thought made me sick to my stomach. When the flower people urged me to eat the cooked scraps, it was a struggle to keep the guilt-free fish from coming up my esophagus.

Each day that passed, the weather grew worse. By the time I put out the fire on the fourth night, the waves roiled to black, with an angry sky overhead.

The familiar paths across the island had disappeared, replaced by waist-high weeds. They tangled around my legs as I walked, and I had to rip the plants out, roots and all.

The fifth day, I finally said, "You know that murder is wrong, right?" I was hoping that they'd understand, that they'd somehow intuit it, like they seemed to do so often. They just stared at me, those black eyes seeming more inhuman than ever. "Murder? Killing people?" Still nothing. "Do you understand me?" I asked, struggling to stay calm.

They had to have a concept of death. Yet they all stared at me like I was trying to explain some alien form of calculus. Then I made things worse.

I strode up to one of them, my Flower Girl, and with both hands, lifted her up by the head. Her feet dangled above the ground, kicking against me ineffectually. "What is wrong with you that you can kill someone and eat their flesh, but you can't answer a simple question? Don't do it. It's wrong, and immoral, and..."

Disgusted, I tossed her aside, watching her body crumple to the ground. I turned to the others. "What in hell is wrong with you?" I roared.

Nothing but stares. Yet there was something else, too. Their confusion had been replaced with—I hate to say it—excitement. That's when I grew scared.

"No," I said, backing away. "I didn't mean... that was a mistake!" They stood still, grinning. "Please."

They took a step forward, collectively. Then another. I didn't wait for the third. I ran for the jungle as fast as I could. I made it, with some difficulty, to a tree, which I started to climb to escape those beings. I have no idea how high I climbed before I managed to find a branch that could support my weight.

That's when I heard the loudest screech, something gleeful yet angry. I hugged the trunk, my breath coming out in only low hisses. The jungle echoed with those terrifying screams. My fingers would have sooner ripped from my hands than let go of the bark. Then, the other screams began.

The other flower people, who didn't hum? No, I realized, it was the wind, the island screaming at me for the wrongs I'd committed. Screams of anger, or grief, or terror—I couldn't tell. It wasn't long until these screams began to wane, and glimmers of light appeared through the jungle canopy. Fires. They were burning the island down, or cooking their new favorite food. My Flower Girl came to mind—the way

     ON THE ORIGIN OF FEAR

her body dangled from my hand before I cast her aside, the way her frame went limp in the dirt. Even if she hadn't died then, the others would have certainly killed her for meat.

◆

An hour or two passed before all went silent again, and the afternoon sky began to fade into evening. I leaned against the tree trunk, hands still gripping the bark for balance. I waited that way for another hour or two, then lifted my head up to see my surroundings. I could see the smoke trails rising ugly and black from fires below, disappearing into charcoal clouds that swirled above. *This is all my fault*, I thought. *If I hadn't shown up, this wouldn't have happened at all.*

Then I saw something in the nearest plume of smoke. A speck of green. Then another speck, of blue, then pink, then scarlet... If I squinted, I could see the flutter of wings, traveling up and away from the carnage. At least the butterflies were able to get away, I thought. Able to leave this miserable island I'd created, to start again someplace new. Five minutes here was too much for creatures that only lived one to four weeks. I decided to do the honorable thing.

I stood up on my perch, my hands shaking while they gripped the tree trunk. I didn't know how high up I was, but I hoped that the fall would kill me. It was too late for me to stop the flower people, but I could still get out. I closed my eyes and felt the wind against my skin, smelled the salt and smoke in the air. I willed my fingers to let go of the tree, my feet to step off their branch. *Go on*, I told them. *It's good, it's over and done with. We're escaping and leaving this Hell.*

They would have none of it. My coward body held still, clinging to the tree with all its strength. I gave up and sat down on the branch again, with nothing to do but watch the thousands of jungle butterflies float off to a better place. I don't know how far they would travel to find new, better land. Some of them would die in midair before they reached it, their corpses dropping out of the sky and into the sea.

◆

After a time, I thought to escape in my little vessel from the *Crescent Moon*. I managed to make my way down the tree and ran towards my boat and my depression and guilt began to leave me. I could already smell the sea, and for once I was desperate to sail; this time, to escape. The foliage started to thin out, and I was smiling as the dirt beneath my feet turned to sand.

My feet started running all on their own, only to come to a confused stop when I reached the spot where I'd washed ashore. I could see the imprint of my little boat in the sand, but all that remained were a few coins and my gun. Everything they could burn, they took. The coins were useless—I reached for the gun. God knew I needed it.

My jaw clenched as my hand closed around the pistol, which was coated with a thin layer of sand and rust. Useless. My senses left me, and I hurled the weapon into the ocean, as far out as possible. The ocean accepted it with a quiet swallow, sending up sea foam like spittle from the mouth of a demented man.

Where to go? What to do? I didn't know, but I was forced to accept that I would remain on this island for the rest of my life. I cried for a few minutes, then decided to find an encampment in one of the caves hidden in the jungle. Yes. I made this island, and I had to live on it.

◆

How have I survived so long? My one advantage over them—strength— keeps me alive. I can fight them off if a skirmish occurs. I live off the fruits that grow high up. Though I've thought of escaping by creating a makeshift raft, I have no tools to cut down any trees.

Whatever driftwood reaches the island is scooped up by those creatures to cook their food. The weather is a continuous nightmare, with hail and typhoons. But as long as I can stay out of their way and endure the island's hateful nature, I can stay alive.

The flower people out there now? I don't call them flower people anymore. They've abandoned their headdresses, and they tear apart any flower they see. I still have the advantage when it comes to strength, but I've noticed something. Their life spans are very short, only ten years or so.

I've lived through three or four generations of these monsters. The newest ones have the same thin bodies and the same bulbous heads as the creatures I once knew. But I swear, they file their nails sharper than any thorn on the island. And once, while I was spying on their camp from one of the surrounding trees, I could see some of the children grinning. They have the teeth of carnivores.

I am afraid.

ON THE ORIGIN OF FEAR

PEDRO INIGUEZ

SIERRA STARFALL AND THE ELDERS OF THE SPACEWAYS

The interceptors, resembling the carapaces of scarab beetles, thrusted through space. The sun glimmered across their frames, illuminating them against the darkness of the void. The patrol ships of planet Hesperia Ultima broke file and fanned out as they pursued the crew of the *Marauder.*

Captain Sierra Starfall gazed out the stern window. She counted four interceptors, shimmering like diamonds in the distance.

"How far now?" she asked, keeping her eyes on the ships.

"We'll enter the asteroid belt in three minutes," First Officer Diablo Caspian said, stroking his long grey beard. "After that they lose jurisdiction to the Prefecture of Beltway Miners."

"They'll reach us before then," replied Helmsman Rags Syntar. His metallic frame swiveled away from the console, turning to Starfall. "They will board us, or shoot us down."

Deckhand Kurt Killborn removed

the straps from his seat, stood, and unclasped his pistol. "They blasted our cannons off when we left Hesperia Ultima. We're sitting ducks." Killborn removed a stray strand of blond hair from his face. "Our only chance at a fair fight is if they board us."

Diablo Caspian unsheathed a short curved cutlass. "We've been here before, Captain," Caspian said, the sparkle of the sword's jeweled hilt matching the fury in his eyes. "We know what to do if they board."

"We wait," she said. "Until they get closer. Killborn—stand by the console and wait for my command. Syntar—keep us on course. Caspian—you can put that sword away."

"What do you have in mind?" Caspian asked.

"We wait until we reach the asteroid belt," she said.

Syntar swiveled back to the helm and nodded. Caspian raised a single eyebrow.

Starfall took a step toward the curved window that wrapped around the ship's stern. She wondered how cold it was out there, in the darkness of space, and about how much pain a body could endure as it floated in the vacuum. She felt the warmth of her breath bounce off the glass as the pane frosted over. When she wiped the

window, the interceptors had closed the distance on the *Marauder*.

A small sparkle, like a pinwheel firework, launched from the tip of the lead ship.

"Captain," said Caspian, eyeing the command screen, "they have launched a concussion missile."

"I see it. Await my command."

She watched the missile as it approached, marveling at its beauty. It twinkled, like the stars in the distance. They reminded her of the countless gems she and the crew had plundered over the years. When they still had luster. When she still cared.

"Captain," said Killborn.

Starfall turned around and gazed through the bow window. The asteroids grew larger by the second.

"Have our escape pods taken any damage?"

"No," Killborn replied.

"Very well." Starfall returned her gaze to the stern. She took the tip of her index finger and drew a smiley face in the frost.

Killborn leaned forward to speak in Caspian's ear. "I know I'm new here," he whispered, "but she's clearly lost it. I say we take over before we're all killed."

Caspian's brow furrowed. "I'd watch what I say, young one. The Captain has a wandering mind, but that makes her no less fit to lead. Starfall always has a plan. Now keep your eyes on that console like you were instructed."

Killborn sneered and returned to his console.

Starfall watched as the missile propelled itself through the dark fabric of space, the twinkle growing into a large fiery blaze with a tail like that of a comet.

"We're approaching the first of the asteroids, Captain," said Syntar.

"Killborn," Starfall said, looking at the moisture on her finger, "jettison one of our escape pods. Aim it at the missile. Syntar, fly us behind one of those asteroids. It should confuse their instruments."

"Y-yes, Captain," Killborn said, tapping in the commands on his console.

Starfall watched on as the *Marauder* shot a man-sized orb directly at the concussion missile.

Just before Starfall could see the impact, the ship cut a sharp turn behind the back of a nearby asteroid. The explosion lit the sides of the rock like the early beams of a sunrise.

"Our scanners show they are returning to Hesperia Ultima," Syntar said. "They think we've been destroyed."

"Good. Now get us to our destination."

Syntar nodded as his hands shifted on the controls.

The *Marauder* weaved through a labyrinth of asteroids, many long abandoned after years of drilling had left them stripped of resources. At least one asteroid, however, still had the signs of a lively mining operation: communications towers springing from the ground like oil derricks, and specks of light running along the landing platforms. Industrial lamps lit the small mining city in a bright blue wash. The long shadows of countless unmanned machines stretched out into nothingness.

As the *Marauder* flew past the northern edge of town, a deactivated drilling rig hung motionless above a two-kilometer wide pit in the ground.

Starfall stared at the darkness below. It seemed to stretch forever. Something unsettling about it, she thought, as the ship sailed past the abyss.

Ahead, a cluster of steel bunkers near the southern edge of town made up the majority of the temporary mining colony.

"Here it is, Captain. Asteroid XB117,"

Syntar said.

"Good," she replied. "We're on time. Land the ship and keep your weapons close. The miners are a rough bunch. Some say isolation has led them to madness."

"We're no slouches in the crazy department either, Captain," said Caspian.

Starfall unsheathed a bowie knife from her belt and traced the edge of the blade with her thumb and index finger. "I know," she said, smiling.

◆

The crew slipped into their pressure suits and attached their weapons within easy reach.

The ramp slid down with a hiss of compressed air. Syntar and Killborn lugged the sealed crates onto the hover-dolly and pushed it forward.

A small tremor rattled the ground beneath them.

"Be careful with the merchandise," said Starfall. "We don't want to spill any."

"I didn't figure this place was known for seismic activity," Killborn said.

"It's not," said Syntar. "There are no tectonic plates. This should be a dead rock."

The door to the nearest bunker opened. Two men in blue pressure suits, armed with power drills, stepped out. The drills made for dangerous close-range weapons and could puncture with ease. Starfall touched the blaster at her side for reassurance.

The guards guided the crew past the airlocks. A loud hiss of compressed air tugged at their bodies.

Inside, a labyrinth of tight hallways and corridors made up most of the bunker. As Starfall walked ahead with the two armed guards, she managed a few glances inside the miners' quarters. They consisted of four rusted walls and three bunk beds stacked together in a claustrophobe's nightmare. Men with scarred faces and missing limbs stared back from the shadows. The hallway wound past more sleeping quarters, lavatories, and a dimly lit game room with a wall rack holding broken pool cues with red tips.

The lights flickered, and an electric buzz—like angered hornets—filled the air. Missing fixtures dotted the bunker, with meshes of exposed wires coiling out of the holes in the walls. Broken slats jutted out of the air-recycling vents along the ceiling.

The guards stopped outside a

spacious mess hall and motioned the crew inside.

A tall, broad-shouldered man in olive fatigues and steel-toed boots stood in the center of the room, stroking his goatee. He tilted his head back as he observed the crew. A long white scar ran perpendicular along his neck.

"Captain Starfall," the man said in a low, raspy voice, "I am Overseer Falkner. I run the day-to-day operations here. I am so glad you made it past the blockade."

"We guarantee delivery," she said.

"So I've heard. The men are about to have dinner. I would be delighted if you joined us. We'll be having stew, biscuits, and grog. Perhaps you'll partake in some of the merchandise with us, as well?"

"The merchandise?" asked Killborn.

"Yes," Falkner said, smiling. "If you wouldn't mind ingesting contraband psychedelic mushrooms with my men that is. They are psychoactive spores emitted from the *Locongo* flower found in the swamps of Hesperia Ultima. When inhaled, they produce a sense of euphoria. On occasion they can lead to strange visions, but I wouldn't worry about that."

"The *Locongo* spores are banned under Hesperia law," Caspian said. "It is a crime punishable by death."

"We have our own laws here. Besides, pirates like you have little regard for the law."

Killborn looked at the crates on the hover-dolly before turning to grin at Starfall.

Starfall smiled back. "Why not? We almost got killed on our way over here. A little stress relief couldn't hurt. Crew, unload the merchandise and get ready for dinner."

◆

Starfall knocked back the mug; bitter, hoppy alcohol sloshed down her throat. She slammed the mug on the table, causing the empty plates around her to bounce.

Across the table, Killborn laughed at a miner's crude joke—his saliva mixing with grog as it trickled down his chin. Beside the deckhand, Caspian sipped his drink slowly, keeping one hand above his cutlass.

Rags Syntar played his electric sitar for the miners. The robot plucked the strings like a spider weaving a web.

All around her, Starfall heard the howls and cackles of revelry. Miners and pirates sat side by side on rotting wooden benches, ingesting the bitter piss-water they called grog. She couldn't help but scowl into her drink. Her darkened reflection scowled back.

"I'm glad you joined us," the gravelly voice behind her said. "Mind if I sit?"

Falkner managed a slight smile.

"Of course," Starfall said.

"Nothing pleases me more than forging strong new relationships. You know, Starfall, certain materials are hard to come by here, with us being so far away from everything. We move from asteroid to asteroid, drilling for resources until we're ready to sell all we've reaped. Thankless work. Hesperia Ultima doesn't thank us. Neither do any of the other planets in the system. All we ask for is some decent food, some entertainment, and the occasional stress relieving... ingredients."

"Plenty of smugglers out there for that."

"We've tried others before."

"What happened to them?"

"Their corpses are probably floating aimlessly through space."

"Well, I'm glad we could help."

Falkner smiled again and motioned to some of his men. A small crew of miners retrieved one of the crates, gently rolling it beside Falkner.

"Shall we?" he asked, unclasping the lid. Falkner grabbed a handful of gray-green sand and threw it up, toward the vents. The pollen danced across the room, swaying in the currents of ventilated air.

The miners shoved their noses upward and inhaled, their chests expanding as the spores filled their lungs.

Killborn mimicked the miners and inhaled with an open mouth.

"What the hell?" Caspian said, placing a hand on the deckhand's shoulder. He closed his eyes and let the *Locongo* spores seep into his nose.

Falkner nodded at Starfall with a devious grin.

She took one last swig of grog. "Screw it, why not?". Starfall stood and sucked in a deep breath. The spores tickled her throat and nose as they shimmied their way down into her lungs.

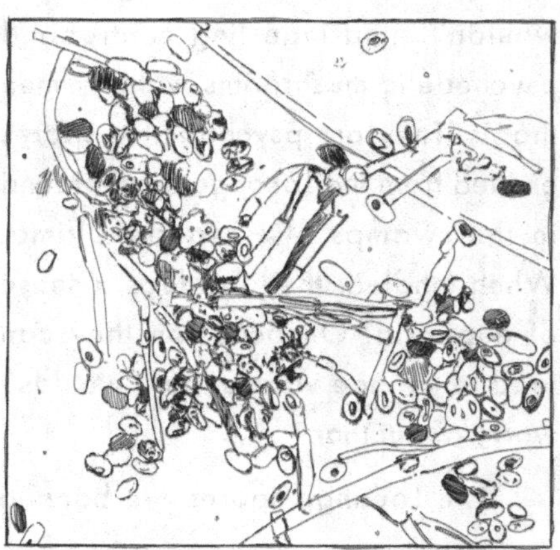

The fungus was odorless, and nearly undetectable.

Rags Syntar leaned against the wall as he played his sitar, the strings reverberating louder than before. The slow twang of steel slithered into her ears and brain, vibrating the universe in a relaxing rhythm.

The miners laughed—a collection of toothless maws and rotten gums, cackling like witches.

Time slowed. Every man in the room emanated a blurry aura. She felt at ease for the first time in a while. Boredom, loneliness—nothing seemed to exist at the moment. Only the sort of peace the dead must feel. Starfall smiled.

Just then she heard something. A subtle banging, like a stick on a faraway drum. Pounding. The sound was muffled like a distant heartbeat.

Boom. Boom. Boom.

Was it her heart? No one else seemed to notice. Was it in her head? Then an ominous sound, like distant ocean waves crashing against rocks. Voices in unison.

"Does anyone else hear that?"

Falkner smiled. This time it was genuine.

"You hear them?"

"I hear *something*," she said.

"Do you want to see them? It's our little secret down here."

She nodded.

"All of you are welcome to see," he said, pointing at her crew.

♦

The tunnel entrance was near the end of the compound, by the equipment facilities. The miners had drilled through dense ashen-colored rock to make the tunnel. It plunged into the darkness of the ground itself. Ragged grooves spiraled through solid rock leading to an unseen cavern. Falkner carried the lantern as he waited for Starfall's crew to enter.

"It's just down there," he said, flashing his teeth like a grinning dog. She wondered if it was all a trap. Was he leading them down there to commit some heinous crime? She shook the thought from her head and continued onward.

The droning grew louder. A humming chorus carrying long notes occasionally broken up by staccato.

"I hear it now," Caspian said, wide-eyed.

"Me too," said Killborn, steadying himself against the tunnel walls. "It sounds like a hymn."

"I hear nothing," Syntar said, shuffling along behind them.

The farther she walked down the tunnel, the more it seemed the walls were closing in on her.

The crew followed her into the darkness, their steps echoing down the hole. The ground rumbled beneath their feet. Loose dirt fell from the low ceiling of the tunnel, bathing them in dust and glittering minerals.

"Damn it to hell," Caspian said.

"Do not despair," Falkner said. "The walls will hold."

Farther down, the tunnel leveled out into a chamber with a path leading to a single wooden door. The voices stopped.

"What's in there?" Starfall asked.

"Take a peek," Falkner said, eyeing a sliding hatch on the door.

Starfall took a step forward. The sound of something shuffling along a dirty floor slithered under the door and into her ears. The *Locongo* flower had disrupted her senses. She felt like she had when sleepwalking as a little girl.

Starfall slowly slid the hatch open. Her gasp echoed into the room ahead

A group of eight gangly humanoid creatures stood from crouched positions and scattered into the darkened corners of the cell. Their skin appeared a muddy-green hue, like that of the amphibians on numerous planets she'd explored. Their mouths reminded her of a piranha's, with tiny needle-like teeth jutting out from a terrible underbite.

Bulbous eyes stared back at her, glistening in the shadows.

She took a step back. Her men rushed to the hatch, shoving their faces against the small window, trying to catch a glimpse. Starfall knelt on the ground, a wave of nausea sweeping over her.

Falkner placed a hand on her shoulder. "'Banu Qasi,' they call them-selves. They came from beyond the belt, beyond the star system. Refugees from some far off, war-torn place. We shot down their ship and imprisoned them here. We give them food and allow them to live as long as they behave and help us with mining."

"Behave?" said Starfall as she fell on one knee, fighting the urge to throw up.

"They are a treacherous lot," he said, running two fingers along the scar on his neck. He turned to Starfall just as she began to gag. "Oh. Captain, you don't look so good. Shall we get you to bed?"

Falkner's cackles echoed down the dark chambers. Then, the world went dark.

Starfall woke on a stiff cot. Her head pounded, and her spine spasmed with every breath she took. Snores filled the cramped, dark room. She peered over the edge of the bed. Below her, the rest of her crew slept like the dead, their limbs splayed out. Syntar set himself on sleep mode to recharge his batteries. Starfall climbed down the bunk bed and stretched.

What had happened? Everything was a blur. The *Locongo* spores. That was it. Falkner said the spores gave one visions. She remembered the sight of green-skinned monsters, hunkered in the dark abyss of a cave, scuttling like vermin against the rocky walls, the nightmare sounds of an ominous hymn, the trembling of the earth beneath their feet. Everything felt like a hallucination.

But had it been? She peered outside the room. The hallway was dim and empty. Only the faint sound of conditioned air blowing out the vents. Starfall stepped outside.

Maybe Falkner would have some answers. She hoped she hadn't embarrassed herself. She would apologize to him for anything her or her crew might have done while intoxicated.

The hallways were long and winding. Nothing, not even the sound of distant footfalls, echoed down the bunker. The mess hall had been meticulously cleaned; any evidence of the night's festivities had been erased.

The temptation to turn back was strong. As was the yearning to revisit what she'd seen. Sierra Starfall had always been a curious woman. Since childhood, her inquisitiveness tended to get her into trouble. No reason to stop now, she thought. She vaguely remembered the way to the tunnel. It was toward the back end of the bunker, near the storage rooms cluttered with busted rigs.

When she arrived it was as she remembered. A long tunnel carved into the earth with what must have been a large drill. She stopped at the entrance of the tunnel, listening for the sounds she'd heard earlier in the night.

Nothing.

Starfall started down the tunnel, running her hands along the walls to keep from tripping in the dark.

She reached the bottom, finding the wooden door where it had been before. Her hands trembled as she slid the hatch open.

Nothing. Just the darkness of an empty cave. Starfall slid the locking bolt and pushed the door open. She drew her blaster, keeping it readied at her side. The cave was cold, and the air was still.

The *Locongo* spores had made a fool of her. They had dulled her senses and clouded her judgement. The miners had probably laughed at Starfall and her crew. *Imbecile pirates, the lot of them.*

Starfall pivoted to turn away when she heard footsteps behind her. She swung around, bringing up the blaster. A group of green monsters stepped out from the shadows.

"Stay right there," she said.

One of the creatures took a step forward. His green skin appeared dis-colored—wrinkled. It opened its mouth, exposing tiny, sharp teeth. It raised a webbed hand in the air.

We mean you no harm. The voice echoed in her mind.

"Who said that?".

The wrinkled creature tapped its chest. *I said that.*

"You can speak into my mind? No, this isn't happening. I must be coming down from the *Locongo* spores."

Your mind is on an open pathway to mine. You have not closed your mind as the others have. My name is Kiak, and I speak for my people, the Banu Qasi.

"No. Impossible. What are you?"

Alive.

"No, no—where do you come from?"

Our history is on the cave wall behind you.

She turned her head, keeping the blaster aimed at Kiak. Behind her, white chalk marks were scrawled over the cave walls. Odd shapes and symbols she couldn't decipher. "I can't read that. Is that your language?"

Kiak nodded. *It is how I keep our history alive. I do it for the young ones,* he said, sweeping a hand over the rest of the group. *I have to erase it every night when the others arrive. They forbid writing.*

"What? Why would they do that?"

Deny them their history, and you exterminate an entire culture's future.

"How did you end up here?"

We are refugees from the planet Qasan, far from this solar system. Our home was destroyed by a people known as the Zurabar. My family and I fled on a small ship. We were crossing this system's asteroid belt when the men of this colony shot us down. We are the only survivors. We are made to toil every day for our survival.

"Slaves."

Kiak nodded.

"I heard singing last night."

You heard our sacred hymns? Your mind must be very receptive. The leader of the men, he can hear us as well, but he closes himself off, resists us, uses torture to silence us.

We sing to the elder god we discovered living on this asteroid. It has become our deity, and it lives here, deep in the abyss. The elders are everywhere, even here.

"The elders?"

Gods born before the universe itself. They listen to us always, and protect us. Though not every elder is known to us, they are there, ever-present. And the elder of this asteroid hears our song every night as it slumbers.

Starfall felt something in her chest. She assumed it was pity. She wasn't sure; she'd rarely forged enough connections to remember what empathy felt like. "I don't know about any elders, but all I know is you can't live like this. I'm sure I can talk to Falkner and arrange something."

We have tried. My son attempted speaking with him. The man you call Falkner ended his existence.

"I saw a scar on his throat. Did your son cause that that?"

My son, in his death throes, reached a hand out, lacerating the man's flesh.

"I'm sorry for your loss, I-"

The earth quaked. The rumble nearly knocked Starfall off her feet. Rocks came loose from the cave ceiling.

"The tremors are getting worse," she said. "What's going on?"

That is the elder. We have been digging too far down into its home. The men refuse to listen. Any moment now the elder will wake from its slumber and break free from the shackles of the asteroid.

"Are you saying this rock is breaking apart?"

Kiak nodded. He took a step back toward the group. One of the Banu Qasi rubbed its stomach. The belly protruded like that of a pregnant human.

"Are you... with child?" Starfall asked.

The Banu Qasi nodded. *I am Onessak. Life will blossom soon.*

"I can't leave you here. It's not right." Outside Starfall heard the faint scuffling of boots on the hallway floor. Perhaps one of the miners on guard. She holstered her blaster. "I'll be back for you soon. I promise." Starfall turned and locked the door behind her.

Through the slit she saw the elder Banu Qasi wipe the cave wall with his hand.

In the quiet of the tunnel, Sierra Starfall began to sob.

◆

She paced back and forth across the room.

"What are you saying, Captain?" Caspian asked. "Those monsters we saw last night were real?"

"Yes."

"I can confirm that," Syntar said. "I witnessed them as well. The spores do not affect me."

"The miners keep them as slaves?"

"That's right."

"Well, what's the big deal? It's not our problem." Killborn rubbed his temples, feeling the full weight of his hangover. "I say we leave 'em."

"Not an option," said Starfall.

"You don't mean we're going to try and save them? That'll get us killed!"

"That's exactly what we're going to do."

"Get killed?" Syntar asked.

"No, save *them*," said Starfall. "We just have to find a way. We're outnumbered here."

"Captain," Caspian said, "we've been through many adventures together. But I'm not sure we can do this."

Starfall crossed her arms across her chest. "We have the luxury of freedom. The luxury of doing whatever the hell we want. Those people down there don't. We're no saints, but we're also not blind. I can't ignore what I saw down there."

The crew fell silent. The sounds of miners rising to shower filled the hallways.

"Well, we've committed our share of wrongs before. Maybe if we do this karma will tip back in our favor," Caspian said. "What do you say, crew?"

Overseer Falkner walked through the doorway. He tapped a blaster at his side. "Good morning, everyone. I hope you all slept well. I couldn't help but overhear—"

Syntar swung his sitar across Falkner's face, the instrument shattering into pieces of wood and steel coil. Falkner collapsed at the doorway.

"I'll get the ship ready," Syntar said. "You just figure out what you have to do, Captain."

"Right. Thanks."

The robot marched ahead.

"Killborn," Starfall barked, "drag his body in here and tie him down. Caspian I'm going to need your help. I've got an idea."

Starfall struggled to balance on Caspian's back as Killborn handed her the crate. She lifted the container and tipped it carefully into the vent.

"We may inadvertently inhale some of the stuff, but oh well," she said.

She poured the entirety of the *Locongo* spores into the vent, the fan sucking up most of the pollen-sized fungus.

"In a few minutes, this structure will be full of armed miners on psychedelics. Stay alert. I'm gonna release the Banu Qasi from their cell." Starfall hopped off Caspian's back and ran toward the tunnel.

"Aye," Caspian said, drawing his cutlass from its scabbard, "we've got your back, Captain."

◆

Starfall ran down the tunnel, her hands guiding her in the dark. The ground trembled and moaned below her boots. She steadied herself against the cave walls until the shaking stopped. When she reached the bottom, she kicked the door open. The wood splintered into a dozen pieces. The Banu Qasi clutched each other's arms as they pressed their backs against the rocky walls of their cell.

"All of you, come with me," Starfall said. "I'm getting you out of here."

Eight Banu Qasi followed her up the dark path. The sound of blaster fire echoed in the distance. At the entrance of the tunnel, Caspian and Killborn, fired their blasters at a group of miners across the hall. At their feet laid three men with crimson slashes decorating their backs.

"Come on Captain, we have to leave," shouted Caspian.

"Lead the way," she said.

Caspian and Killborn charged ahead, shooting wildly. The smell of ozone and singed flesh was overwhelming. Starfall covered her nose with one hand. As she turned, she saw the Banu Qasi clearly for the first time under the halogen lights. They had no noses. Their skin was moist and semi-transparent. Their naked torsos were marked with sedimentary streaks like camouflage. Open bruises oozed across their flesh like the pox. She felt a wave of pity sweep over her again. But, more than anything, she felt purpose.

An alarm rang out across the compound, blaring through hidden speakers. The white lights switched to a deep red. The sound pierced her ears and drilled through her head. Beads of sweat dripped down her forehead.

Starfall couldn't tell if the ground was quaking again, but her feet trembled all the same. The spores were disrupting her motor functions.

The crew sprang down the maze of hallways, running past the dining hall and the run-down rec room.

Suddenly, a miner thrust out from one of the sleeping quarters as Starfall marched past. He tackled her to the floor, his hand reaching for her blaster. The man had a small crater where one of his eyes used to be. His one good eye, aggravated by the spores, was bloodshot and furious. Who knew what visions danced through his head?

The miner wrested the blaster from her grip. Starfall shot a hand down her thigh and unclasped the bowie knife from its sheath. The man pointed the blaster at Kiak. Starfall raised her knees and bucked the man slightly forward, disrupting his aim. She plunged the knife into his side. He spasmed on the floor like a fish before dying.

Above, Kiak offered an outstretched hand. Starfall accepted it and smiled. He heaved her up and placed a hand on his chest before bowing slightly.

"Are you alright, Captain?" asked Caspian.

"Come on," she said, ignoring the question "we're close to the entrance."

The vents hissed and spat out a fine ashen dust. A few miners sat with their faces buried in their knees, rocking back and forth as they succumbed to the psychedelics.

Ahead, the entrance door was sealed.

"Damn," Killborn said. "We don't have a way of opening it."

"No pressure suits, either," said Caspian.

The loud, furious shriek of machinery buzzed behind their backs. Falkner stood in a pressure suit, cradling a power drill like a rifle in his arms. The large drill bit spun in a dizzying blur. Falkner eyed the group of pirates and slaves with rage. His visor had fogged, obscuring most everything but his eyes.

"You monsters aren't leaving alive," Falkner said, raising his drill. "I should've known you spacers were planning some treachery."

Caspian and Killborn raised their blasters. Falkner slapped his wrist. The doors slid open. Depressurized air tugged at Starfall's clothing with a hiss. The cold vacuum of the asteroid's atmosphere yanked the crew and the Banu Qasi off their feet and sucked them outside like rag dolls. Starfall clung to a set of guard rails on the wall.

Falkner slapped his wrist again and the doors sealed shut.

Starfall dropped to the floor. The world spun. Slowed down.

"I want you to do me a favor, Captain," Falkner said, stepping forward. "In your last breaths I want you to describe what this feels like."

The drill spun again, buzzing like a colony of bees. Starfall crouched low to the ground, her legs coiled like springs. In the corner of her eye, she spotted it, glistening like the jewels that used to catch her fancy. Caspian's cutlass.

Falkner's stride turned into a full gallop. He raised the power drill to chest level and jousted for her midsection. Starfall snatched the cutlass and took a step back toward the entrance door. She drew her arm back, preparing the cutlass for a downward blow. If the drill caught any part of her flesh, she'd be torn to shreds. She would have to dodge at the last second and swiftly counter to one of Falkner's limbs.

Her head pounded. The spores in full effect. Falkner's body warped into a distorted combination of colors and shapes. *Focus.* The sound of the drill. It grew closer. A few feet away now. She readied the blade. Falkner lunged forward. Her legs bent slightly. Now or never.

Just then, the ground quaked. The floorboards cracked apart and the ceiling tore open, cables spilling out like guts. Falkner lost balance and momentum carried him forward. The drill sailed past Starfall's head and lodged itself in the door. As Falkner tried to pull it out, Starfall took a quick step back to give herself some room and brought the cutlass down on his forearm.

Clean cut. His right arm dropped to the floor.

Overseer Falkner let loose a howl barely muffled by his mask. Starfall kicked in the back of his kneecap, and the overseer dropped to the ground. She drew the blade back and brought it down on his neck. The screaming stopped.

Starfall dropped the blade and inhaled a deep breath of air. She closed her eyes to stop the shaking in her mind. When she opened them, the floor lay in ruins. Asteroid XB117 was on the verge of collapse. She looked around. The crew! She reached for Falkner's severed arm and pressed the button on his wrist. The airlock doors slid open, tearing apart the drilling tool. The vacuum pulled violently at her body. She let herself be yanked away. She landed outside, skidding on the rugged ground.

She gasped for breath as the chill air stung her skin like a million needles. Her crew was nowhere to be seen. She closed her eyes and waited for the darkness to take her. She'd laughed in Death's face before. Now it was time for Death to collect on her bounty.

Above, the loud whir of thrusters burning through the air. The *Marauder* swung low, ramp extended. Caspian and Killborn were at the end, hands outstretched. She stood and took both. They hoisted her up and walked her up the ramp before it sealed shut behind them. Clean oxygen flowed through her lungs.

The Banu Qasi approached Starfall and formed a circle around her. They bowed their heads and embraced her gently. Like family.

Below, deep fissures splintered across the asteroid, splitting the terrain apart.

"Syntar, get us out," yelled Starfall as she turned to her helmsman. The robot nodded.

The *Marauder* shot vertically, thrusters at full power. The Banu Qasi lost balance, spilling over like bowling pins.

A massive sinkhole opened beneath the colony. The facility's communication towers collapsed as the ground gave way and the structures were drawn into the dark depths below. The crew could make out a few tiny specks trying to escape the compound—the miners were swallowed by the dark maw like ants in a flood.

"Look, Captain," Caspian said, pointing out the bow window. All around the *Marauder*, hundreds of asteroids began to crack apart. Wide fissures zigzagged across their rocky exteriors. Their surfaces exploded, shooting plumes of sediment into space.

Nestled inside the core of every exposed asteroid sat what appeared to be large transparent spheres filled with a gelatinous substance. Starfall rubbed her eyes. The spores were still manipulating her mind. Had to be.

Two black ovals pressed against the inside of each membrane. Some even seemed to be tracking the *Marauder's* flight. Suddenly, as if orchestrated, the sacs burst, the liquid shooting off in every direction.

Hundreds of ancient anomalies stared at the *Marauder* as they hovered in space. Their bodies were like that of baby chicks: long, pointed beaks; bulbous, milky-black eyes; naked wings wrapping around their bellies. They looked... premature. Like things neglected by nature and left to die.

They have woken, Kiak said. He

  SIERRA STARFALL AND THE ELDERS OF THE SPACEWAYS

stared in awe, a hand reaching for the air in front of him. The Banu Qasi kneeled and bowed their heads. The crew sat in silence.

"Are you seeing what I'm seeing?" asked Killborn after a time.

Caspian stood alongside him, placing a gentle hand on Killborn's shoulder. "Aye, lad. Aye."

Some of the birds began to move their heads and uncoil their once-cramped wings. Others lay motionless, floating in a lifeless drift as starlight lit their stillborn bodies.

"Some of them are dead," said Starfall.

"A result of the mining operations," Syntar said.

"Yeah. Something tells me we woke them early."

The Banu Qasi began to chant. An ancient prayer to ancient beings.

"Give us some room, Syntar," said Starfall. "Move us slowly away from here." Syntar nodded. The *Marauder* jetted away.

The birds that were still alive craned their necks, their heads gazing curiously at the passing ship. One by one, they extended their limbs and drifted slowly apart in every direction. Birds the size of asteroids. Starfall couldn't believe it. Could anyone?

"Imagine how beautiful they would have been," she said looking upon the stillborn elders floating in the void. Starfall looked upon the Banu Qasi as they held hands in prayer. Life went on. Starfall turned toward the chicks still spreading their wings. "And yet... imagine how beautiful they will be still."

ELENA SICHROVSKY

MARIGOLDS IN WINTER

The doctors have a long, fancy name for it, but Danny and I just called it "the drippies." We had a big talk about it at our school in the summer, where we had to sit on the basketball court for an hour and look at these icky pictures on a slideshow that kept showing Danny's shadow fingers. He put them up against the light whenever they showed something yucky.

They called it a virus, and said us kids catch it because we're still growing. I'm not growing as fast as Danny though, he's gotten like five centimeters taller since his birthday. And now he says we can't pair up for the three-legged race because I'm too short and too slow.

First you will get tired, the warning poster said. We had to bring one home to our parents, and Danny poked out the eyes on the picture's face so we could wear them like masks. I folded my poster into a cup so I could collect some marigolds petals to float in water like tiny boats.

Then, because the virus makes you not feel like drinking, you might have to get a big needle in you to put food in your body. Like smoothies, my sister

MARIGOLDS IN WINTER

Teresa said, except you won't be able to taste them. The last thing to happen, when you know it's too late to go to the doctor, is that you start to melt down, like a snowman but slower and not as thick. It's more like banana milk that's frozen but getting mushy again.

That's what they said would happen if we caught the virus but then it didn't always go that way, because one day at lunch Stella was complaining about the weird mustard her mom put in her burger and then she saw her fingers oozing into the bread. We had to end class early that day, they made all our Moms or Dads come pick us up and I didn't even remember Dad's phone number. I just know that he and Mom work at the hospital so they were probably busy helping all the kids. Danny's mom took me and Teresa home instead.

But then it happened to Danny, when he was practicing with his new friend Jonathan for the three-legged relay race. I saw him sweating a lot, like big drops I could catch and smear on my pants. Then his face looked like it fell off when he fainted on the track. His forehead and cheek were all gone, but I helped to collect some in my hands and bring it to the school nurse.

After that day the school closed, and all the kids went home or to the hospital.

I was in the hospital for awhile, with Teresa and even my baby sister Cassie was there. We got the needles in us, and Mom kept trying to make me drink water or juice but even though I like orange juice I didn't feel like drinking it those days. Except for when the nurse came to change the bags that the needles go in. I really wanted to know what the see-through liquid stuff tasted like. Does someone else get to try it, like the doctor?

We aren't in the hospital anymore. It closed after too many kids came and there was no more medicine. The doctors said we could just go home and rest for awhile. They didn't know how to fight the virus because it was everywhere in the air. But at home Mom and Dad still have medicines, and they give it to us every day, two or three different kinds. Sometimes their friends give them new ones to try, like a special spray that was supposed to make our bodies hard and not mushy. But it made our skin too hard like rocks and we couldn't breathe. My chest felt so heavy until Mom washed it off.

She told me I wouldn't get "the drippies" because all the needles and medicine were making me grow slower. But then one day I woke up and my pillow was all crusty, like a smashed bowl of cake batter and the crumbs got stuck under my nails when I tried to scratch it out. I went to brush my teeth and saw my right ear had dripped away to the floor, and some ooze was still dripping out of the side of my head.

Some science people said the virus is in the air, so they are trying to fix that. They are working on building special suits for us to wear. Teresa and I tried one, but as soon as Dad helped us put it on, our legs started to squeeze out between the cracks like toothpaste in little squishy squiggles. I tried to smash them back in, but it just got all over my hands, sticky like a pack of taffy left out in the sun too long.

Teresa is more sick than me now. She has to wear a special hat because half of her head fell off when she rolled out of bed. I almost slipped in the puddle when I was going to the bathroom, it was all white and red and she was lying there screaming. But now she has a glass hat like a helmet—Dad says it's to keep her brain inside. Before, her brain used to look like the pictures in my science book, choppy like ketchup on mashed potatoes. I like to put lots and lots of ketchup on my potatoes, and then mix it up and splat it around the plate until it's a pink sauce.

That's how Teresa's brain looks right now.

But yesterday Mom said they finally found a new medicine that will really work well, and it won't need needles. That's good because I don't like needles. One time I asked her why she doesn't have a needle that can just put me to sleep, like I heard them talking about how Danny's parents did. That made her look sad, or maybe mad, and she sat down next to me. Danny's parents got in trouble for doing that, she said, because until our whole body turns into soup the virus is still active and can spread to other people or animals and plants. Maybe it can even go into the earth itself and the whole planet might get "the drippies" and we would drip right off! It sounded scary and so I asked Mom where would we go if we turned into a big puddle of goo and she said the people in charge of the country made a special place to keep us.

I call it the Freeze Factory. I saw it once on TV when Dad thought I was sleeping. It looked like a big factory with freezers inside and people were standing outside in line with their kids in buckets and bowls and some had a bathtub! I bet the science people were going to study them inside the Freeze Factory. I told Mom she would probably need two buckets to carry me over because even though my stomach got all shrunk and my arms are thin,

I think I grew some more inches, and maybe I'm as tall as Danny now.

That made her look even more sad or mad and she hugged me so tight my chest started to feel mushy and she had to let go. And she promised me that she and Dad would never take me or Teresa or Cassie to the Freeze Factory. That's good because me and Teresa really don't like the cold. Summer is our favorite season.

Today we're going outside for the first time in a long time because the man with the new medicine is meeting Mom and Dad there. Dad carries us to the car and we get to take off our bandages, all the soggy white strings. Some of them crusted stuck on our bones and Mom had to use warm water to pull them off. I bring my science book so I can find some of the flowers in there. I've memorized the long names of all thirty-two flowers in there, that's more than Teresa. She only knows twenty, but since having to wear the brain hat she only remembers five and even then she says the names all wrong.

Baby Cassie starts squealing when Mom puts her on the grass in the park. She's trying to eat it and I keep taking it out of her hands. I think she doesn't know she can't eat it but I know what everything is. It's brighter outside than I remember from before but most of it is still the same. Trees are tall and itchy, but now most of their leaves have gotten brown and fallen down. The grass is wet and pokey, and there are some bees watching over the flowers, like soldiers guarding a palace of treasure. Teresa is sitting there smiling, or maybe her jaw is slopping off, but she seems to like the leaves I put in her hands. They stick to her body like the star stickers I used to get on my chart in school for getting the answer right.

I can see Mom and Dad talking with a man and he's giving them gloves to wear and a long gun. I saw people do that before in a movie, wearing gloves when they creep into the dark room to catch the bad guys. I think we're going to play pretend. We haven't played in a long time.

"Go look at the flowers, " Mom tells me. "See who can count more petals."

My legs are too gooey to stand on so I wriggle through the grass. There are some daisies, a few morning glories, but they each only have a few petals. I'm going to count the marigolds because they have the most. Cassie is face down in the dirt, her ears turning into little pools next to her. She has no chance to win for sure. Teresa is just sitting there, staring ahead. She's probably counting in her mind but that's cheating.

I make sure to count mine out loud, pointing at each petal to show that it's mine. "Fifteen, sixteen, seventeen...."

I can hear Mom crying, or laughing. She does both when she's excited. The new medicine must be so good that we can stay in the park for awhile and play pretend. "I want to be the bad guy!" I shout. "But, before you start looking for me you have to count to one hundred so I can hide. And no peeking, okay?"

She and Dad are standing at the flower bed next to ours, a bit far away, and she's putting something round into the gun. Just like that game Danny had on his phone. When his Assas-ain Two got to Level Nine he got this super gun that could shoot not just bullets but bigger bombs. He could shoot just once and explode things into a hundred pieces.

When Mom sees me looking her eyes get crazy big and she starts screaming at me. "Don't look, Julian! The flowers, how many have you counted? Take your sister's hand, help her count, do it now!"

I don't want to help Teresa beat me, but I see Dad kneeling on the grass, covering his face. He must be mad at me and Dad is never mad at me. So I try to take Teresa's hand but my fingers are too soft they can't even move, they just splat down. I use my other hand and grab Teresa's, pointing it at the daisies, but all I feel is mush squeezing from my fist. Her thumb squirts between my fingers and plops down onto the petals.

"Mom, Teresa is going drippy." I turn back to see her kneeling next to Dad and pointing the gun at us.

"Don't look, Julian, don't look! Look at the flowers!" She's not laughing. She's crying. Her whole face is crying. I don't know this pretend game. So I pick some flowers for Teresa to help her win and put them in her lap. The yellow and orange colors float there in the puddle of her legs along with some of my fingernails.

I tell her something from my science book to help her remember the flower name. "Did you know, Teresa, that marigolds grow in winter too?"

 MARIGOLDS IN WINTER

Mom keeps saying the same thing over and over, as if I don't understand her. "Look at the flowers, baby. Look at the flowers."

I think she would be happy if I gave her some flowers too. I choose two yellow ones for her, but my hand slips off my wrist just as I snap the stem.

And then I hear something in the gun go click.

AUSTIN P. SHEEHAN

A SONG FOR GANYMEDE

Smooth as molten silver, the *Luxembourg* maneuvered through the asteroid field, destination Ganymede. Our mission was simple: fill her external water tanks and return to Mars. From the comms station, I watched the captain smile as her eyes absorbed the vista before us. Not only was this the *Luxembourg*'s maiden voyage, this was Stella Jensen's first mission as captain. Everyone at the Wassermann Transport Company had watched her rise through the ranks, becoming one of the youngest WTC captains in the company's short history. Some employees had started measuring time by her promotions, not years.

♦

A light on my station flashed amber. A distress beacon. Captain Jensen's eyes darted at me, her dark hair tied back in a bun.

"I'm scanning for the source," I said, typing into my console. *Probably some miners in trouble on a dead asteroid.* Before I could lock on, the signal disappeared. "It's gone."

"Officer Walther, cut speed by thirty percent."

"Done," said Walther. A conceited smile spread across his face.

Again, the amber light lit up my station. "Let's not lose it this time, Keller," Jensen said.

"I'm doing another scan." My fingers flew across the console, fixing onto the beacon. "Found it! A ship, low orbit on the far side of Ceres."

"Good work, Keller."

"There's a recorded message, Captain." I glanced up. Our eyes locked for a second.

"Well, play it."

I keyed the command, and a distorted voice filled the bridge. "*This is Ta— the Eagle I. If you're receiving this... please help. Our ship... damaged in— teroid field. Small family of— Ganymede-bound. Going into stasis. Hope... the... —rt holds.*"

Everyone's eyes were on the Captain.

"Walther, change course," she ordered. "And decrease speed. We're going in for a closer look."

◆

Their ship filled the viewscreen. An old Yankee-class transport with a small cargo bay. But unlike the *Luxembourg*, the *Eagle I* was capable of going inter-atmosphere. Or would have been, if she wasn't so damaged. She spun slowly on her axis, her hull dented and scarred, gaping holes in her side. Our scans indicated she was still using power, but all systems were off-line.

"What do you think, Captain?" whispered Suun, our shy systems engineer and medical officer.

"I think this just became a rescue operation." She turned to face us, eyes keen. "We're going to dock with them. Check their crew, their cargo. If they can make the trip safely in stasis, we'll take them with us."

In silence, Walther matched speeds with the transport while the cratered surface of Ceres filled the viewscreen.

Jensen turned to me. "Comms Officer Keller, don't you have a job to do?"

"You want me to communicate with a crew that's in stasis?"

"We're about to initiate an orbital docking procedure. And we're going to do it by the book."

"Okay, Captain." I shook my head. *What kind of response did she expect?*

"*Eagle I*, this is WTC transport *Luxembourg*, do you read? Over." Silence.

"*Eagle I*, this is the Wasserman Transport Company's *Luxembourg*, do you read? Over." Walther was barely concealing his laughter. Even Suun sported a rare smile.

"*Eagle I*, this is the *Luxembourg*. Wakey-wakey. We're about to perform an ODP. If you could stop your rotation so our Nav Officer doesn't have to do all the work, that'd be appreciated." I looked up at Jensen with a shrug. She was not amused.

"Match their spin, Walther," she ordered, as I removed my headset.

Walther maneuvered the *Lux* with grace, deftly controlling her thrusters. It was a delicate operation; a blast at the wrong time and we'd collide. As much as Walther's smug arrogance got to me, he was an impressive pilot.

"Docking procedure complete," said Walther.

"Good work," said Jensen, her voice calm. "Walther and Keller stay here. Everyone else—get suited up." As comms officer, I had to stay at my console, but envy wormed through me. Just once I wanted to suit up and explore the unknown. Space got boring watching from behind a monitor.

♦

"Captain, what do you see?" I asked into my headset. I wasn't getting anything from their video feeds.

"Darkness. Every system's out except the stasis pods. We've got three survivors."

"They must be the luckiest sonsof-bitches," I said, turning to Walther.

"For an asteroid to take out all power but the pods, that's unheard of..." A chill ran up my spine as his voice trailed away.

"I've got a bad feeling about this, Captain. Be careful."

"There's no danger," dismissed Suun's soft voice. "The *Eagle I*'s hull has ruptured, but she's holding."

"She's right," Jensen added. "There's no other signs of life, and very little in the way of cargo. We're going to bring their stasis pods aboard the *Lux*."

"Are you sure that's a good idea, Captain?"

"We have to. Her stasis pods could fail any moment, and she'll be under even more pressure when we start moving again." I glanced at Walther, who gave a resigned nod.

"Roger that, Captain." I put down the headset and turned to Walther. "What are you thinking?"

"I think you need to talk some sense into your girlfriend."

"Jensen and I aren't—"

"Oh that's right—she dumped you." He grinned, enjoying picking at my old wound.

     A SONG FOR GANYMEDE

"It was a long time ago, and I'm over it," I said. "Anyway, she won't listen to me."

"That's probably why she's doing so well these days," he mused. He was a great pilot, but was even better at pissing me off.

♦

"Captain, are you sure about bringing them on board?" asked Walther, when Jensen returned to the *Lux*'s bridge.

"Something doesn't add up about this, Captain," I said. "No Yankee-class ships have left Mars recently, and Ceres has only just come between Mars and Jupiter. She shouldn't be out here if she's going to Ganymede."

"I know. It strikes me as odd, too." Jensen sighed, looking from face to face. "But we all know the Planetary Space Council law. Any ship that is capable must respond to a distress beacon. Any crew trapped on a damaged ship must be rescued. I'm not going to break PSC law in my first mission as captain, dammit! So unless you have anything helpful to contribute..."

"Space is a lot more dangerous, and a lot more unpredictable than the halls of the Academy, Captain..." My face burned as I realized what I'd said. *Shit.*

"Officer Keller," Jensen replied with a withering look, "I'm beginning to regret requesting your services for this trip."

"Sorry, Captain. I didn't mean that how it sounded."

"It'd be easier to accept that apology if you weren't the Communication Officer. Route your systems to my console. You're dismissed."

Overcome by embarrassment, I slunk off the bridge, Walther's laughter following me down the steel hallway.

♦

I found Suun in the auxiliary cargo deck with the *Eagle I*'s stasis pods. Each pod had an ID card pinned to a small storage compartment. We stood next to each other, staring into the faces of the *Eagle I*'s crew, who wore nothing but black underwear. Our guests were: Aquil, a thin, muscular, dark-skinned man with greying hair; Liani, a petite woman in her early twenties, with long light-brown hair and a smile on her lips; and Tarek, was a young man, stocky with strong features and dark curly hair.

"How are they, then?"

"They all appear healthy." Her voice barely carried over the humming of the *Lux*'s engines. "But I'm having trouble accessing their vitals. That can happen after moving active pods, and should sort itself out soon. But I don't see it, Keller."

"Don't see what?"

"The family resemblance." She was right. They all looked different—different bone structures, skin tones, hair colours.

"What are the odds that an asteroid would take out all systems except the stasis pods, Suun?"

"Maybe not all other systems..." A thoughtful expression crossed her face. "It might have been a malfunction, but my scanner detected something else draining power. I couldn't trace it though. Regardless, Life Support systems like stasis pods are the most heavily protected. But having all the other LS systems out except the stasis pods... I've never heard of anything like it before."

"I think there's something wrong about all this." They couldn't just be lucky. No one was that lucky.

"Do you think it could be some kind of trap?"

"I'm not saying that, but..." I shrugged.

"Not possible, Keller. We're in the middle of Planetary Space Council territory. No one would set a trap here. Maybe on the far side of Uranus, but even then it'd be unlikely. Plus, the crew are in stasis. They won't wake up until we tell them to. They pose no threat whatsoever."

Reassured by her words, and relieved of my duties, I went to my bunk.

◆

Jensen was waiting for me in my quarters. Not the good kind of "waiting," where she'd be under the covers, wearing nothing but a smile. "Charlie, we need to talk." She was wearing her tank top and leggings, sweaty from a workout.

"Sure thing, Captain." I stood to attention. "I apologize for what I said earlier."

She continued, ignoring my apology, "How long have we known each other? As friends."

Friends? We were definitely more than that at the beginning. "About seven years, Cap– uh, Stella."

"I've known you the longest of anyone on board. And you're right. The Academy taught me a hell of a lot, but not everything. When I graduated, they told me I had a habit of always making the right decision. Everything in the book—every damn thing I've been taught—says bringing that crew on board was the right call. So why do I feel like I've done the wrong thing?"

　　　　A SONG FOR GANYMEDE

I stood there silent, unsure what to say. It had been years since the confident, determined Captain Stella Jensen had been so open with me.

"I can't—"

BANG—a shockwave shook the ship, answering for me. The lights flicked out and the doors shut, sealing us in.

"Shit! What was that?" I said.

"Shh, listen!" The fire alarms had kicked-in—a shrill beeping echoed through the ship—but no klaxons warning of a hull breach.

"We can't have hit an asteroid—Walther's too good for that."

"Shut up, Keller. Walther and Suun are on the bridge. They haven't called for help. No intercom, no radio..."

"Which means?"

"We've got to get to the bridge!"

Jensen typed a security clearance code into the access panel while I grabbed a torch, my heart racing. The door slid open, revealing the *Lux*'s dark upper hallway. The alarms blared, but we didn't hear shouts or footsteps. Faint wisps of smoke floated above us as we crept toward the armory. Jensen unlocked the weapons safe, passing me a blaster rifle and taking two pistols for herself.

"What's the plan?" I asked, trying to keep my voice from shaking. I was scared. I was the comms officer—this was not in my job description.

"Let's check the cargo bay on our way to the bridge, Charlie. Stay calm, okay?"

I nodded. "Should we radio the bridge?"

"No. Come on, let's do this." Nausea welled up inside me as we descended the ladder into the main hallway, still hearing nothing but the alarm. *What were we getting ourselves into?*

Approaching the smoke-filled auxiliary cargo bay, Captain Jensen and I glanced at each other and cocked our weapons.

Through the smoke and flickering light, we could see the stasis pods. Jensen nodded, and I turned on the torch, my hands shaking. The back of one pod had been blown off, exposing burnt-out electrical circuits. Both were empty.

"Why would they blow up one of their own pods?" I asked.

"Some stasis pods can be programmed to open in the event of emergencies. Damn. I should have seen this coming."

"They set this up—it's a trap!"

"Come on, we need to get to the bridge." Jensen jogged ahead.

I swallowed my fear and followed.

Jensen crouched in the doorway, anger flashing in her eyes.

"Come on, Charlie—I need you!"

"I bet they're waiting for us," I said, the blaster rifle shaking in my hands.

"Probably. Breathe, okay?" She looked into my eyes. "Charlie, we've got this. Just don't shoot unless they shoot first."

"Wait, they've got to be Earthers!" I said, my fears finally finding their voice. Earth. The very word sickened me. Radioactive clouds, ruined cities. Nothing but death and misery remained. Its only inhabitants were dangerous criminals from the colonies, or the Earthborn—descendants of people too damaged by the radiation to leave. People only went to Earth, no one ever came back. It was a death sentence. If the *Eagle I* was from Earth, her crew would be deadly.

"Earthers? But only PSC Police transports have clearance to travel to or from Earth."

"I know, but the Yankee-class is old. Some could still be hidden down there from before the prohibitions."

"And that would explain why they were at Ceres," nodded Jensen. "Flying from Earth to Jupiter, Ceres would have been right in the way." That made sense. Too much sense. "I'm still going to want you to wait till they shoot before firing back, Keller."

"Understood." I knew I wouldn't have to wait long.

◆

Jensen opened the door, revealing the bridge. Suun and Walther sat in their seats, but my attention was drawn to the figures in dark shipsuits, grins on their faces and blasters aimed at us. Tarek's mouth twisted into a sneer when he saw my gun. His was bigger.

"Welcome," said Aquil, with a friendly smile. "Which of you is the captain?"

"I am," said Jensen. "Who the hell are you, and what do you think you're doing on my ship?"

"Of course. I'm Aquil, and my comrades are Tarek and Liani. We don't want anyone to get hurt, so I suggest you lower your weapons."

"And I suggest you tell your people to lower their weapons, unless you want the back of your head sprayed over the viewscreen." I'd never seen her like this before.

"We're the ones with hostages,

not you!" snarled Tarek, aiming his blaster at Walther's head. My weapon trembled in my sweaty hands. *How was Jensen going to play this?*

"You want your ship back, and your crew alive," Aquil said, voice calm.

"And what do you want?" asked Jensen, tightening the grip on her pistol.

"We want your help," said Liani, turning from the viewscreen and sweeping her hair behind her shoulders, a smile on her face.

"Our help?" I spluttered in disbelief. "We already rescued you and your ship!"

"Yet what choice did you have?" A smile stretched Aquil's lips. "Not having done so would have violated Planetary Space Council law. So now is when you can *choose* to help."

"And if I don't, you'll execute my crew."

"Perhaps."

"Okay, aside from saving your lives, what else do you bastards want?" Jensen asked.

"We need you to deliver us and our cargo to Ganymede's Azny dome."

"Hang on," Walther said, his voice defiant, "that's where they're trying to recreate Earth, isn't it?"

"Indeed," nodded Aquil. "They've got Earth trees and crops growing in the thousands of tons of soil they've transported over."

"Not possible. That's the hardest place in the system to get into," said Suun, her voice soft but firm.

"It's ironic, isn't it?" asked Aquil, "They've recreated the perfect environment for humans, but won't let any in."

"Who are you, and why do you want to get to Azny so bad?" demanded Jensen. Aquil and Liani shared a glance. "No bullshit. Are you Earthers?"

"No. We're from Mars."

"The Captain said 'no bullshit!'" I snapped, forgetting my fear. "If you were coming from Mars, why were you in orbit around Ceres?"

"We are from Mars," said Liani, her voice hesitant. "We just took a detour via Earth."

"I don't believe that." Jensen spat in disgust. "No one goes to Earth for a goddamned visit! Tell the truth."

"You didn't search our cargo bay, did you?" sneered Tarek.

"We did," said Suun. "Not much there. Food supplies. Martian bullion."

Aquil smiled.

"Okay. What did we miss?" asked Jensen.

"The first rule of running a transport business is there are always hidden compartments. If you find ours, you'll find your answers."

"Why don't you Earther bastards just tell us?" I asked, turning to Aquil. "We'll be more likely to help if you're not feeding us bullshit."

"Earthers?" asked Liani, turning to me. "What do you—could you—know of Earth?"

"I know it's a radioactive wasteland. I know no one who goes there is allowed to set foot on another colony again." I tightened my grip on my blaster rifle.

"Look at us." She stepped forward, her blue eyes bright and clear. "Do we look like escaped prisoners? Do we look like radioactive freaks?"

"Look at that ugly-ass piece of shit in front of you," I said, nodding at Walther. "He doesn't look like the best pilot in the system, but he is." Walther stared at me, a slow smile spreading across his face.

"Setting a trap and hijacking whoever sprung it would be high up on the to-do list of goddamned Earthers too!" snapped Jensen.

"Indeed. But first, Earth is not the wasteland you think it is," said Aquil. "Small pockets of life endure— small islands in the Pacific. While the wretched mass of humanity—or what was humanity—tears itself apart, birds still announce each new morning with their song."

"Birds?" Walther whispered. I held my breath, transfixed by the thought of the long-extinct creatures.

"Fish, lizards, and insects, too." As Aquil continued, a radiant smile lit up Liani's face. *What was he saying?*

"If they aren't dead, the radiation...," said Jensen.

"We scanned them. They're clean."

"Not possible," muttered Suun.

"See for yourself!" said Aquil, closing the door on Jensen and me.

◆

"They're bluffing," Jensen said, pressing her back against the cold steel wall.

"It's impossible," I agreed. "But what if—"

"They're selling us a dream, Keller. Everyone wants the Earth to be reborn, to have the animals back. But they're gone." She sighed, dejected. "We need to focus. They have command of the *Lux*. If we go to the *Eagle I* we'd be relying on them to let us back in."

"You're right, Captain. And with us searching the wreck, who knows what

A SONG FOR GANYMEDE

they might do to the *Lux*, or to Suun and Walther. We can't risk it."

Taking a steadying breath, Jensen opened the doors again. "No deal, Aquil."

"Well, we tried to make it easy for you," said Tarek, aiming his gun at Suun's head. "But we don't need to make deals."

"You're wrong," I said. "You can't get to Azny without us."

"Why? We can land this ship as easy as any other."

"No—she's an orbiter," said Walther, some sense of pride returning. "She can dock at space stations, but can't land planetside. Hell, she'd probably fall apart under any atmospheric pressure." Liani and Tarek's faces fell, and they turned to Aquil.

"You've got dropships. Landing craft."

"We do, and I control those from here," said Walther, sitting up in his chair. "I can get you to Azny's front door in one, if you want to get there so bad."

"One of us can pilot it from here," said Aquil.

"Any of you had training with I-270 Autohoppers? They aren't easy. Are you willing to put your lives—your cargo— in the hands of someone who doesn't know what they're doing?"

Aquil glanced at his crew. Liani's face was creased with concern. "Our best chance is to convince you to help us," he conceded.

"I'll go." said Liani, hopping to her feet and walking toward us.

As the door hissed shut behind Liani, she lowered her empty hands with a warm smile, ignoring our blasters. "It was pretty tense in there, hey?"

"Tense? You could say that," Jensen growled. "Taking over a ship at gunpoint... Give me a good reason why I shouldn't just kill you now?"

"You'll have your reason," she said with confidence, walking toward the cargo bay.

"This shit just gets weirder and weirder," I said.

"You go into the *Eagle I* with her, Charlie. I'll stay on board the *Lux* and make sure they don't do anything to my ship. Liani looks harmless, but don't be fooled. They're dangerous."

"Don't worry about me," I said, swallowing hard.

◆

Captain Jensen sealed the *Luxembourg*'s airlock behind us. Walther had docked one of our external airlocks with theirs, forcing both open, creating a hallway between our ship and theirs where Liani and I stood, in our EVA suits.

"Are you excited?" she asked. "We were on a tiny island in the middle of the ocean when I saw them."

"They're so beautiful—you'll see. And... I was torn. The Earth is dying. It won't be long before that last healthy part is gone forever. Aquil said we have to save them, and Azny is the only place they can have a future. But getting them there will be hard—anyone from Earth would be shot on sight, and with this cargo, where else could we be from?"

What was she saying? It was all so impossible, and I was already struggling to breathe inside the heavy EVA suit.

"It'll be okay," she said, noticing my discomfort. "Follow me."

Liani opened the *Eagle I*'s inner airlock, and I activated my suit's torch. It was dark, but we could see tools and equipment floating in zero gravity. We activated our grav boots, and I followed Liani into the darkness, gripping the blaster in my gloved hands. She walked fast, sure of her destination and unhampered by her suit. She didn't even stop to look through the holes in the hull at the terrifying blackness of space. I was out of my depth, just struggling to breathe in my EVA suit. What had Liani seen, to casually stroll through a wreck like that?

She was waiting for me in the cargo bay. As my torch revealed her EVA suit in the darkness, my heart skipped a beat—she held something in her hand. Something long and metallic. *Shit!* She was armed. That's why she walked here so fast! She grinned as she pointed the weapon at me.

No way was I going to let her take me out. Her face fell as I squeezed the trigger of my blaster rifle, firing wildly. Flashes of incandescent light filled the cargo bay.

Shit.

◆

I opened my eyes, shining the torch around the cargo hold. Her pale figure was still in front of me. The chest of her suit had dark burn holes, and drops of liquid floated behind her. *Shit.* If it wasn't for her grav boots, she would have been thrown against the wall. My heart hammered in my chest as I stepped closer, still clutching the blaster tight. I caught her eyes, staring at me through her faceplate. Dark blood—almost black—floated from her mouth, hovering inside her helmet.

Liani didn't look scared as her life left her. As the light of her blue eyes faded, she weakly nodded to the wall panel near an access hatch.

A SONG FOR GANYMEDE

Floating in front of her was a harmless steel tube.

Shit.

I approached the wall panel, hoping like hell the secret compartment was close. My stomach had turned to water. I'd screwed up. No matter what happened now, Aquil and his crew would kill Walther and Suun, probably Jensen, and definitely me. *Shit.* My hands shook as I reached for the panel.

If I couldn't find what they hid, I'd have killed an unarmed woman for nothing.

I pressed hard against the panel. Nothing. I leaned close, looking for a concealed mechanism that might open it. There was a slight groove inside the recessed edge—that had to be it! My heart raced as I ran my finger over the groove. Nothing. There had to be some way of triggering it. The tube—Liani must have grabbed it for a reason! I grabbed it, and looked it over.

One end was welded shut, just thin enough to slide into that gap. I took a breath and pressed the welded end of the tube between the panels. Yes! The panel popped out, just half a centimeter. This was it! Heart racing, I let go of the tube and pulled at the exposed edges. It was stuck. I couldn't pull it out any farther. I tried to slide it, and found it spun. I twisted it halfway around and pulled again. Holding my breath, I slid the panel out and a pale blue glow filled the cargo bay.

◆

"What happened?" asked Stella—*Captain Jensen*—through the airlock's intercom, as I returned alone.

"I fucked up, Stell." My voice shook.

"Where's Liani?"

"I... I killed her."

Her expression changed from disbelief to hopelessness.

"Damn. Now they're going to kill Walther and Suun. Fuck. Why the hell did yo—"

"It was an accident. But listen, Stella—they're telling the truth. I found the storage compartment. We've got to help them."

"What did you see?" she asked, a glimmer of hope in her eyes.

"I saw the impossible." I shrugged, hardly able to believe it myself. "So what are we going to do?"

Jensen tested the weight of the blaster pistols in her hand. "Charlie, tell me what happened in there. Why the hell did you kill her?"

"I fucked up. I let her get ahead of me. She reached the cargo bay first. When I caught up, she had something in her..." I sighed, unable to meet Stella's gaze. "I thought she was armed. I thought she was going to kill me."

"It's okay, Charlie," she said. A lie. It wasn't okay. It was a mistake that could mean our deaths, and we both knew it. "What happened after that? What did you see?"

I took a deep breath. "Okay. This is going to change everything."

◆

The door hissed open, and we were face-to-face with their blasters.

"What did you do to Liani!" demanded Tarek, dark eyes full of rage.

"Don't shoot!" I said, heart pounding, my arms shaking in the air. "It was an accident. But I saw it. We'll help you."

"Walther, Suun—are you okay?" shouted Jensen from the doorway. We couldn't see anything behind Aquil and Tarek's solid frames.

"You killed Liani." Tarek stared into my eyes. "You've gotta pay."

"No!" Aquil shouted.

Helplessly, I watched the barrel of Tarek's blaster rise, his face contorting in hatred and rage. Then his head exploded in a shower of shrapnel and sparks. Tarek was a robot, no— an android!

"A goddamn bot," Jensen grunted, turning her blaster on Aquil. "I'm more than happy to kill you, too. So if you want to live, don't do anything stupid." Her eyes darted around the bridge, and her face fell.

I looked past Tarek's crumpled body. Suun sat crumpled in her chair, eyes glassy.

"No more death," said Aquil, raising his blaster above his head. My eyes stayed locked on Suun, and my heart sank. A trail of blood from under her dark hair trickled down her neck, down the front of her shipsuit. She finally found something she couldn't fix.

"You killed Suun and Walther!" growled Jensen, through clenched teeth.

"Walther is merely unconscious," said Aquil, his voice heavy. "Tarek killed Suun. He was hurt by Liani's death." I glanced at Tarek's body, steel cables and coloured wires where his head should have been, dark oil oozing out onto the floor.

"How did you know?" I asked, as Walther groaned.

"We are androids, as you've discovered. Pz-12s, manufactured on Mars by Z.T. Industries. We can communicate, and share data wirelessly. She—Liani—she stopped communicating."

"Pz... I've not heard of your model before," said Jensen, stepping forward and taking Aquil's blaster rifle from his hands.

My mind raced. Escaped androids could be more dangerous than Earthers, but Aquil was calm, even remorseful. What was going on?

Aquil sat down heavily at the comms station. "We're new, and it's dawning on me that we may be significantly flawed."

His voice was bitter as he watched dark oil pour from Tarek's body and the smell of shorted circuits filled the bridge.

"Captain, just shoot the bastard," said Walther. "Do it for Suun."

"Keller saw what they're carrying. They weren't lying. We're going to help." A smile—just electrical circuitry—lit up Aquil's face.

◆

"Ganymede Orbital, this is the WTC transport *Luxembourg*."

"This is Ganymede Orbi—"

"Ganymede Orbital, this is the Wasserman Transport Company's *Luxembourg*, do you read? Over."

"WTC *Luxembourg*, we re—"

"Mayday, Mayday. This is WTC *Luxembourg*. Ship is malfunctioning." Through the airlock I saluted Captain Jensen. I had no idea what this might cost her, but I had a good idea what it would cost me.

"Please respond, Ganymede Orbital, this is the WTC *Luxem—*" My pre-recorded message was cut off as the airlock sealed, locking me in the autohopper with Aquil and our cargo. I forced a smile as I belted myself in, arms trembling.

"You don't have to do this, Keller," said Aquil.

I shook my head, "I do."

As I answered, I yearned to return to the *Luxembourg*. But, getting that cargo into the Azny dome was everything.

"Keller," Jensen's voice sounded strained over the radio. Had she changed her mind? Was she going to order me back on board? Honestly, part of me hoped she would. "Good luck, Charlie. I'll miss you." I nodded. *I'll miss you too, Stella.*

"Prepare for launch." My stomach turned to ice as Walther's voice sounded through the intercom. "You're crazy for doing this, you know?"

"We know," my voice croaked. "Anyone putting their life in your hands needs their head checked."

"Don't test me, Keller. Autohopper launch sequence engaged." I swallowed hard, trying to concentrate on my breathing. "Five. Four. Three. Two."

The 'hopper jerked sideways, then dropped toward Ganymede. My stomach felt like it stayed with the *Lux* as we fell, the autohopper trembling around us.

"I hope Walther is as good a pilot as you said," shouted Aquil, over the 'hopper's engines.

"Me too!" If we blew this landing, we'd be screwed. Correction: we

were screwed anyway. But if Walther pulled through, we'd have a chance of making this worthwhile.

"Keller, what happened to Liani? Is that why you're coming, because you feel responsible?"

"We're all doing this because of your cargo," I said, looking into his eyes. "But yes, I feel like shit for..." My eyes dropped to the floor. "I didn't want to kill her. But I thought she was armed. I thought..."

Aquil placing a firm hand on my shoulder. "Her last message was *forgive him*." I swallowed, overwhelmed by guilt and sadness.

When I regained my composure, I asked a question that had been on my mind since Tarek's head exploded. "What were you doing on Earth, Aquil? And, you're robots—how are you all so different?"

"To make the Pz-12s seem as human as possible, the designers tried something different. Instead of only positive traits and unquestioning loyalty, they based our profiles on both positive and negative traits of different Zodiac signs. Liani was a Libran: kind and gentle, but also unreliable and laid back. Tarek was a Taurean: patient, dependable, yet stubborn, possessive and prone to anger." Aquil paused,

 A SONG FOR GANYMEDE

thinking about his lost comrades.

"It was Tarek who convinced us to escape," he continued. "He knew we could pass for humans, and I knew that we could do so much more than the mindless tasks they gave us. We crash-landed the *Eagle I* on a tiny island on Earth. The PSC ships flew past when they saw us, thinking we were doomed, that we'd never fix her. And they were right, in a way." The 'hopper shook violently. If he said anything else I didn't hear it - the scream of the engines and the increasing g-force pushed me back into darkness.

◦

"Wake up!" yelled Aquil over the roar of the engines.

"What's happening?"

"We're slowing do—"

CRUNCH. The 'hopper lurched to a shuddering, sudden halt, throwing us forward against our restraints.

"Are you okay?" I nodded, pain bursting through my chest. We unfastened ourselves then checked the cargo. The automated airlock extended with a whirr, locking onto the Azny dome. Alarms filled the air, and I grew nauseous. As the 'hopper forced open the dome's airlock, I promised Walther I'd buy him a beer if I ever saw him again. Removing my helmet, I breathed deeply as the oxygen-rich air filled the 'hopper.

"No one move!" A guard stepped through the airlock, blaster drawn. *That was fast.*

"I suggest you stand aside," smiled Aquil, firing a blaster rifle, burning a hole through the guard's neck. *Shit. This is it.* Adrenaline surged through my body, I grabbed a blaster and ran out of the airlock into the Azny dome.

"Cover me, Keller!" shouted Aquil as he followed, dragging the cargo.

Underneath the blue-tinted dome was a massive open space, filled with trees and buildings. In the distance were vast fields.

"Drop your weapon! Put your hands in the air!" Behind me, Aquil was struggling with the cargo case. A squad of guards crouched behind a security barrier, not fifty meters in front of us. To the left and right, more guards were moving forward, trapping us.

There was nowhere to hide. I raised my blaster to fire, to give Aquil the extra time he needed. As my finger reached for the trigger, I saw Liani's face, breathing her last breath, asking me why.

A burning sensation ripped through me. I fell to the ground screaming.

As the laser blast burned a hole through my stomach, I convulsed in agony. Overcome by the searing pain, I could only watch as three more blasts flashed above me, toward where Aquil was struggling with the cargo. We had failed.

Aquil groaned as he fell, dying on the surface of Ganymede. *All because he had a dream.* I looked up at the massive orange ball in the pale blue sky. There wasn't any pain anymore, just coldness. As my vision faded, I caught a blur of movement. A flash of deep blue, a hint of green. Then, breaking the silence, a sweet and high sound I'd never heard before.

No, not a sound. A song.

A SONG FOR GANYMEDE

COVER ART:
ALYSSA ALARCÓN SANTO

Alyssa Alarcón Santo is a freelance illustrator based out of Portland, OR, where she lives with her writer husband. Her love of meticulous hand lettering, cynical philosophy, and all things literary are common threads in her artwork. When she's not busy working as *Planet Scumm*'s creative director, she can be found creating commercial illustration work for clients like National Novel Writing Month.

She's currently working on a fiction comic inspired by her close Mexican-American family.

While Alyssa often works digitally, swearing by the easily-transportable combination of an iPad Pro and Procreate, she also has an impressive (read: excessive) collection of Posca paint pens. She loves to draw subjects that are detailed, structural, and, dare I say it, even a little tedious. (We all need our Jerry Gergich.)

Her work can be found online at alyssasantodesign.com or on Instagram at @alyssasantodesign.

PLANET SCUMM: What science fiction apocalypse scenario scares you the most?

ALYSSA ALARCÓN SANTO: Before this last year, I probably would have said a 1984 style "believe not what you see" society. Nowadays, I have to say 2020s every-dystopia-at-once approach is the true waking nightmare I never considered.

PS: How do you know when you're done with an illustration?

AAS: I don't think you ever truly "finish" a piece of artwork per se. You just do your best to get the concept across and rein yourself in before you overwork it.

PS: What's the best artist advice you've read or received?

AAS: I have repeatedly faced the hard lesson that when you're learning, you're always going to suck for awhile. I always *needed* immediate mastery and if I ran into the necessity of practice, I would drop the thing. Drawing was something I idly wanted to pursue as a kid—my parents are both artists so it's in the genes—but I always felt I couldn't because I wasn't naturally great at it.

I picked it back up in my early 20s and even though I genuinely sucked, I loved illustration so much that I stubbornly committed to learning for the first time.

Turns out, the only secret to mastery is repetition. Repeat the movement until you understand why the thing you're trying to do works. Apply that knowledge and repeat until the movement you sucked at feels easy—then you move onto the next thing.

PS: What scientific advance do you most eagerly await?

AAS: I have a fervent, unrealistic hope that robotic body attachments and/or enhancements happens in my lifetime. I'm disabled and don't walk well so robot legs are the dream.

PS: What helps you get through quarantine?

AAS: Drawing, creative competition reality shows, and being quarantined with a wonderful partner.

PS: What gives you hope?

AAS: Science.

COVER ART: ALYSSA ALARCÓN SANTO

SPOT ILLUSTRATIONS: SAM RHEAUME

I've retreated from my year of travel because of *cough* well... you know.

After landing home I have moved to a hidey hole back in Vermont with my three-legged dog and my partner, Nicole. I now eat a lot of cheese and am doing very little to prevent myself from getting fat. But that's 2020.

When I'm not drawing, I'm listening to Jens Lekman records or reading about the evolution of Eastern Orthodoxy after the collapse of the Byzantine Empire or wondering how Fastball ever gained traction even in the world of gratuitous 90's radio rock.

More of my work can be found on social media at @sirheaume or at samrheaume.com.

♦

PLANET SCUMM: How do you know when you're done with an illustration?

SAM RHEAUME: It locks into the idea you had for it and the notion of adding more detail begins to feel pointless; whenever the idea communicates clearly in the language you've decided to use.

PS: Lycanthropes or vampires?

SR: Lycanthropes. So much has been done to revise the vampire, root out it's classist narrative, sexualize its bloodlust, mourn its lonely immortality.

The werewolf, on the other hand, is always fleshed out as a little more lowly, a condition that is a cyclical nuisance. I'm going with them because there's a real proletariat tale waiting to be told.

PS: What's the best artist advice you've read or received?

SR: I had an art professor tell me, "Sometimes you just have to be a dumb painter. Save your thinking for after you're done. While you're painting, just be dumb about it."

I remember this when all the narrative and anxiety creeps in before or during an illustration or a design or anything in life, really.

PS: What helps you get through quarantine?

SR: Wine, dogs, and working.

PS: Who would win in a fight, a giant squid or three polar bears?

SR: I foresee a bloody draw. But then, right before the credits roll, we get a close up on the lifeless squid eye which suddenly swivels in its socket to look directly at the camera.

How many sheep would an Android dream if an android could dream sheep?

SR: One high-output assembly line's worth.

PS: What gives you hope?

SR: Oh man.

 SPOT ILLUSTRATIONS: SAM RHEAUME

SUBMIT TO PLANET SCUMM'S SPECIAL ISSUE

SNAKE EYES

On *Planet Scumm*, we want to read stories that are different and unexpected. Stories that introduce new ideas, or that look at old ideas with a fresh perspective. And while we like to think that *Planet Scumm* is a space where historically marginalized writers can be heard, we also know there's always more work to be done to support representation in sci-fi and speculative fiction.

That's why, for *Planet Scumm #11: Snake Eyes*, we're asking for submissions from *cisgender women, transgender women, transgender men, non-binary people, and genderqueer people*. We kindly ask authors who don't identify along those lines to not submit to this call.

FIND THE FULL GUIDELINES AT PLANETSCUMM.SPACE